ONE FOR THE MONEY

Mitch drew his Remington and performed a fancy spin. "See this, redskins? I've got ten dollars that says I can draw and blow out your wicks before you so much as lift a finger."

"They're not bothering anyone. Let them be," Fargo said.

"What do we have here?" Mitch asked no one in particular.

Fargo came up off the bench more swiftly than a striking rattler. Mitch belatedly stabbed for his hardware but he hadn't quite cleared leather when Fargo swept the Colt up and out and clubbed him across the temple.

"Anyone else?" Fargo demanded.

THE
TRAILSMAN

#261

DESERT
DEATH TRAP

by

Jon Sharpe

A SIGNET BOOK

SIGNET
Published by New American Library, a division of
Penguin Group (USA) Inc., 375 Hudson Street,
New York, New York 10014, U.S.A.
Penguin Books Ltd, 80 Strand,
London WC2R 0RL, England
Penguin Books Australia Ltd, 250 Camberwell Road,
Camberwell, Victoria 3124, Australia
Penguin Books Canada Ltd, 10 Alcorn Avenue,
Toronto, Ontario, Canada M4V 3B2
Penguin Books (N.Z.) Ltd, Cnr Rosedale and Airborne Roads,
Albany, Auckland 1310, New Zealand

Penguin Books Ltd, Registered Offices:
80 Strand, London WC2R 0RL, England

First published by Signet, an imprint of New American Library,
a division of Penguin Group (USA) Inc.

First Printing, July 2003
10 9 8 7 6 5 4 3 2 1

The first chapter of this title originally appeared in *Blood Wedding*,
the two hundred sixtieth volume in this series.

REGISTERED TRADEMARK—MARCA REGISTRADA

Printed in the United States of America

PUBLISHER'S NOTE
This is a work of fiction. Names, characters, places, and incidents either are
the product of the author's imagination or are used fictitiously, and any resem-
blance to actual persons, living or dead, business establishments, events, or
locales is entirely coincidental.

The Trailsman

Beginnings . . . they bend the tree and they mark the man. Skye Fargo was born when he was eighteen. Terror was his midwife, vengeance his first cry. Killing spawned Skye Fargo, ruthless, cold-blooded murder. Out of the acrid smoke of gunpowder still hanging in the air, he rose, cried out a promise never forgotten.

The Trailsman they began to call him all across the West: searcher, scout, hunter, the man who could see where others only looked, his skills for hire but not his soul, the man who lived each day to the fullest, yet trailed each tomorrow. Skye Fargo, the Trailsman, the seeker who could take the wildness of a land and the wanting of a woman and make them his own.

Nevada Territory, Summer 1861—
Deceit, danger, and death at every turn.

1

Over a low rise to the east appeared a young maiden, running as if her life depended on it. Long raven hair streamed behind her as she swiftly descended a game trail. She moved with the natural grace of an antelope, a comparison heightened by the buckskin dress that clung to her lithe form.

Skye Fargo was about to saddle up after a good night's sleep when he spotted her. He watched with keen interest, enticed by the flash of her shapely legs. She was so intent on running, she didn't spot his camp hidden in the brush less than a stone's throw from the bottom of the rise.

The reason for her flight became plain when three men sprinted over the top.

Fargo's lake-blue eyes narrowed. The trio were also on foot, which in itself was remarkable. No one in their right mind tried to cross the high desert country between the Great Salt Lake and the Cascades without a horse. Even more peculiar was the fact that one of her pursuers was white, another red, and the third black. "What the hell?" he wondered aloud.

The white pursuer wore just about the silliest outfit Fargo ever saw, a two-piece affair that resembled bright red long underwear. Bushy sideburns and a thick mustache framed his pale face. His gait was as odd as his appearance; he loped in a long, stiff-legged

1

motion, attended by the windmill pumping of broom-stick arms.

Next was a husky Indian more sensibly attired in a breechclout and knee-high moccasins. Fargo couldn't be completely sure at that distance, but it sure looked as if the warrior was an Apache. Which was preposterous. Apache territory was many leagues to the south.

Last came the black man. A strapping specimen, he wore a pair of faded jeans and a floppy brown hat that hid half of his ruggedly chiseled face. He didn't seem to be exerting himself all that hard yet he had no trouble keeping up with the others.

The maiden looked back, saw them, and ran faster.

Fargo didn't know what was going on but he wasn't about to stand there and let the men catch her. Experience told him they had to be up to no good. The maiden dashed past his camp without a sideways glance. Dropping his bedroll, Fargo turned toward his horse. The Ovaro was twenty yards away, slaking its thirst at a small spring. He intended to mount up but a quick look showed the three men were already near the bottom of the rise.

Impulsively, Fargo hurtled from the scrub brush. He thought it would be easy to intercept the three before they overtook their quarry. But he gave them too little credit. Once on flat ground, they had doubled their speed.

Fargo was in excellent condition, his sinews hardened to iron by a life in the wild, his stamina second to none. He settled into a long stride, the jangle of his spurs a constant reminder that he might have been better off using the Ovaro.

It pushed Fargo to his limit but bit by bit he narrowed the gap. Soon he was only thirty yards behind. Then twenty. Then ten. He could see beads of sweat on the back of the black man's neck when, alerted by the sound of his spurs, the man suddenly glanced over his shoulder. Seconds later the Apache did the same.

Last to hear, the gaudily garbed white man twisted around.

"Hold it right there!" Fargo bellowed. He was almost on top of them and about to palm his Colt when he realized, to his considerable amazement, all three were unarmed. But they were far from defenseless. The black man whirled and cocked a fist the size of a sledgehammer. Only Fargo's razor-sharp reflexes spared him from a broken jaw.

"Mr. Samuels, no!" the white man bawled, but the big black man paid no mind.

Fargo dodged a second blow, and a third. He landed a solid jab to the gut that would usually double a man over, but the man merely grunted. Whirling to dodge a flurry of jabs, he glimpsed the Apache, standing aloof. The white man's mouth was agape. At least they weren't lending a hand.

Samuels was nothing if not determined. He waded in again, his fists flying.

It was all Fargo could do to keep from having his head knocked off. He blocked, ducked, then delivered an uppercut that jarred the bigger man onto his heels. In the blink of an eye, Fargo had his Colt out and leveled. "Enough!" he barked, thumbing back the hammer. "Simmer down or you'll eat lead."

Undaunted, Samuels raised his arms again but the jasper in the red outfit grabbed his wrist.

"Be sensible, my good fellow! Let's get to the bottom of this before you resume pummeling him." He had a British accent as thick as jam. To Fargo he said, "I demand to know the meaning of this unjustified assault, sir."

"Unjustified?" Fargo repeated.

"What else would you call it?" Samuels angrily growled. "You had no call to come rushin' up on us like you did."

Fargo nodded at the maiden, who had stopped and turned about sixty feet ahead. "We'll let the girl you

3

were after be the judge of that." He beckoned, and after a few seconds of hesitation she jogged toward them.

"Do you know Swift Fox?" the Englishman inquired. "Is this some unfathomable lark on her part?"

The Apache had folded his muscular arms across his broad chest and showed no inclination to join in the talk.

Samuels, though, shook a calloused fist. "If this throws us off the pace, I'll report you to the officials! And take it out of your hide, to boot."

Fargo never liked being threatened. "You're welcome to try."

"You talk mighty big when you're holdin' a six-shooter," the black man snapped. "Why don't you holster it and we'll see just how tough you really are."

"Now, now, Mr. Samuels," the Englishman cautioned. "Violence is the last resort of the feeble-minded."

"Are you callin' me stupid? Just because you're some high-falutin' lord muck-a-muck doesn't give you the right to insult folks."

"I am an earl, not a lord," the Englishman curtly replied. "I wish you would bother to remember that." Facing Fargo, he gave a slight bow. "Earl Desmond Sherwood, at your service. I trust you will overlook Mr. Samuels's tantrum. He has them with distressing frequency."

Samuels opened his mouth to say something but fell silent at the arrival of the gorgeous maiden with the lustrous black hair. She also had an effect on Sherwood and the Apache. The former drew himself up to his full height and smoothed his thin patch of russet hair. The latter ran his gaze up and down her shapely figure like a hungry man who craved a feast.

Fargo touched his hat brim. Up close he could tell she was a Crow, which was as strange as everything

4

else. The Crows lived a week's ride or better to the east. "Do you savvy English?"

"I speak your tongue quite well, thank you," Swift Fox said, her enunciation superb. "Why did you attack these men?"

"I saw they were after you and figured I'd lend a hand." Fargo drank in the beauty of her smooth complexion, dazzling dark eyes, and teeth as white as the purest snow.

"You thought they meant to harm me?" Swift Fox regarded him with heightened interest. "That was noble of you. But your help was not needed. They pose no threat. They would not risk being disqualified."

"Hear that, did you, mister?" Samuels rasped. "You made a jackass of yourself for nothing. We're practicing, is all."

Thoroughly confused, Fargo lowered his Colt. "For what?"

Desmond Sherwood took it on himself to answer. "Why, the great race, of course. The First Annual Nugget Chamber of Commerce Test of Endurance in the Art of Footracing. With a grand prize of ten thousand dollars."

A couple of years ago a rich vein of silver had been discovered down near the California border, and ever since, prospectors and others hoping to get rich quick had been scouring the mountains and deserts for more. Whenever a new strike was made, a new settlement immediately sprang up. Nugget, as Fargo recollected hearing, was one of the latest in a long string.

"They've been vigorously promoting the event for four or five months now," Sherwood related.

This was the first Fargo had heard of it. He twirled the Colt into his holster. "My mistake."

"And that's it?" Samuels prodded. "You pull a

damned hogleg on us and expect there won't be any hard feelings?"

"Forgive and forget, what?" Desmond Sherwood said. "It was a simple misunderstanding. I'm satisfied." He smiled at Fargo. "Perhaps you should give some thought to attending the festivities. Head due east and you can't miss the town." Squinting up at the sun, he declared, "We're wasting valuable training time, lady, gentlemen. Shall we press on?"

And just like that, the four of them resumed running, Swift Fox once again in the lead. As they departed Fargo noticed the most remarkable fact of all. Even though the ground was littered with countless stones that could cut flesh to ribbons, she was barefoot.

Wheeling, Fargo hiked back to the spring. The notion of paying Nugget a visit appealed to him. He had been on the go for over a week, traveling from San Francisco to Cheyenne. A day or two of cards, whiskey and women, not necessarily in that order, were just what he needed.

By the middle of the morning the temperature had climbed into the nineties. Fargo pulled his hat brim low against the harsh glare of the sun and held the pinto to a walk. The arid landscape baked under the sun's onslaught, fit for lizards, snakes and scorpions, and little else.

Fargo shifted in the saddle. Swift Fox and the others had long since vanished into the haze. He shook his head and clucked to the Ovaro. Anyone who went running around in that heat had to be loco, ten thousand dollars or not. He wouldn't do it for twice that much.

Their tracks were as plain as the buckle on Fargo's belt. All he had to do was backtrack to their starting point. What he found was yet another surprise in a day chock full of them.

Nugget was no sleepy mining camp. It had buildings

and hitch rails and water troughs, its streets crowded even in the heat of day. Banners had been strung, and somewhere a piano was playing.

A festive air held sway. Everyone Fargo passed on his way in either smiled or cheerfully bid him welcome. As he drew rein and started to slide down, a portly man in a suit and bowler barreled toward him with a pudgy hand thrust out.

"Greetings, stranger! Welcome to our grand celebration. I'm Mayor Jonathan Quinby." The mayor had the grip of a soggy sponge.

"What is it you're celebrating, exactly?" Fargo asked. "The footrace?"

"Heard about that, did you?" Quinby hooked his thumbs in his vest. "But the race is only a small part of the overall proceedings." He had droopy jowls that quivered as he spoke, and cheeks worthy of a chipmunk. "I take it you haven't kept up with the news, then?"

"I've been on the trail a while."

"Ah. Well, surely you've heard about the creation of the Nevada Territory? Not that long ago President Lincoln appointed a territorial governor. And Nugget has been officially recognized as a town." Mayor Quinby puffed out his chest like a rooster about to crow. "We're celebrating with two full weeks of frolic and fun. The footrace is the highlight but by no means the only activity planned."

Fargo scanned the streaming currents of contented humanity. "Everyone sure seems to be having a good time."

"And so should you, my friend, so should you!" Quinby always talked as if he were on the stump. "Many of our businesses are offering discount rates for the duration, and there's free beer every evening from five until five-thirty courtesy of the chamber of commerce."

"Your town will go broke before this is over."

7

"I beg to differ, sir," Quinby said earnestly. "Our coffers are swollen with revenue from the silver mines. Why, how else do you suppose we can afford a cash prize of ten thousand dollars to the winner of the foot-race and two thousand to whoever comes in second?" He puffed out his chest even more. "It was my brainstorm, I'm proud to say. Races are all the rage in places like Denver and Saint Louis. And there's one down New Mexico way that annually draws thousands of spectators."

Fargo had witnessed the New Mexico race a few years ago, and he agreed it was a crowd-pleaser.

"Perhaps you would care to enter?"

"Me?" Fargo chuckled. "That'll be the day."

"Why not? The entry fee is only a dollar. And you certainly look fit enough. I daresay you might give the favorites a run for their money." Quinby laughed at his little witticism.

"How many are running?"

"Fifty-seven. We hope to have sixty by race time the day after tomorrow. You can register at the Quinby Hotel or other places."

"You own the hotel?"

"Just one of them. And one of the banks. And several other businesses. It's safe to say no one has more clout in Nugget than I do. If I can be of any help to you in any regard, you have only to ask." Doffing his bowler, Nugget's leading citizen scampered off to greet someone else.

Fargo spied a group of ten or eleven Crows across the street. Relatives and friends of Swift Fox, he reckoned. He decided to stretch his legs. There were the usual assortment of townspeople, prospectors, miners and gamblers, plus more than a few curly wolves. Hardened gunmen and the like, hovering like hawks looking for something to kill.

Although it wasn't yet noon the saloons were open and doing a brisk business. Fargo pushed through bat-wing doors and shouldered through the noisy crowd to the bar. He paid for a bottle of whiskey, then searched in vain for an empty table. Venturing back out, he sat on a bench in the shade of the overhang, tipped the rotgut to his mouth and let it sear his insides. It was the real article, not the watered down excuse resembling coffin varnish some establishments served. Fargo smacked his lips in appreciation. About to take another swallow, he paused.

Two Apaches were coming up the boardwalk. Mimbres, unless he was mistaken, the same as the Apache runner he had encountered. They wore headbands, long-sleeved shirts, and pants, over which they wore breechclouts. An Apache custom, as were their knee-high moccasins. One cradled a rifle, the other had a bow and quiver slung across his back. Both had big bone-handled knives on their hips.

Fargo had nothing against Apaches, nor against any other tribe for that matter. He had lived with various Indians from time to time, and learned that just like whites, there were good ones and bad ones.

Pedestrians gave the duo a wide berth. No outright hostility was shown, just a wariness born of instinct. The warriors were like wolves among sheep, and the sheep knew it. Most of them, anyway. For as Fargo looked on, four toughs who had been lounging against the saloon straightened and planted themselves in the path of the Apaches.

"Lookee here!" declared a scrawny excuse for a gunman whose Remington had notches on the grips. "More mangy Injuns! It's gettin' so a fella can't hardly turn around without trippin' over one."

"They're worse than lice, Mitch," commented a man with straw-colored hair. "What say we squish 'em just for the hell of it?"

A third hitched at his gun belt. "Count me in, Harley. The only thing I like more than stompin' redskins is spittin' on their graves."

The Apaches had halted and were waiting for the whites to move out of their way. Their faces betrayed neither fear nor worry.

Mitch spread his legs and placed his hands on his hips. "How about it, you red devils? Care to oblige me and my pards? We'll buck you out so fast, your heads will spin."

"Look at 'em!" Harley scoffed. "Standing there like bumps on a log. Hell, I bet they don't understand a lick of English." He poked the foremost warrior. "Come on! What does it take to rile you lunkheads?"

Passersby were stopping to stare. An elderly rider reined up and leaned on his saddle horn. No one seemed particularly eager to intervene.

Mitch drew his Remington and performed a fancy spin. "See this, redskins? I've got ten dollars that says I can draw and blow out your wicks before you so much as lift a finger."

Harley laughed and poked the foremost warrior a second time. Again, neither Apache reacted. They might as well have been sculpted from marble.

Fargo took another swig of whiskey. The goings-on had nothing to do with him. He was better off sitting there and minding his own business. Butting in would only land him in trouble he didn't need. So why, then, did he hear himself say, "They're not bothering anyone. Let them be."

All four gunnies turned. Mitch and Harley swapped glances and sauntered toward him, side by side.

"What do we have here?" Mitch asked no one in particular.

"One of those good Samaritans the Bible-thumpers are always gabbin' about." Harley snickered. "How about if we show him what we think of his kind around these parts?"

Fargo treated himself to another long swallow, wiped his mouth with a sleeve, and commented without looking up, "Go play in the street before I forget how green you are."

Harley bristled like a riled porcupine. "Mister, you're about to lose half your teeth." He hiked his boot to kick.

"You first," Fargo rejoined, and came up off the bench swifter than a striking rattler. He slammed his knee into Harley's groin and the straw-thatched gunman folded with a whoosh of expelled breath. Mitch belatedly stabbed for his hardware but he hadn't quite cleared leather when Fargo swept the Colt up and out and clubbed him across the temple. The other two were too stupefied to do more than gawk as Fargo leveled the Colt and demanded, "Anyone else?"

Some of the onlookers were in a state of shock. Others seemed pleased the young quick-trigger artists had been given their due.

The Apaches hadn't moved a muscle. But now, without a word of thanks or any acknowledgment of the favor Fargo had done them, they stepped around the gunmen and walked on.

Fargo didn't care to stick around. Nugget was bound to have a lawman and he had better things to do than spend half an hour answering a bunch of nuisance questions. Keeping one eye on the gunnies, he backed up until he came to an alley. Wheeling, he went through to the next street and turned left. People were everywhere, all in fine spirits. Overhead was a bright yellow banner that read: TODAY A TOWN, TOMORROW A CITY.

A few blocks farther Fargo came to a quieter saloon. To while away the time he sat in on a game of five-card stud. One of the players was as gabby as a gossipy spinster and rambled on and on about the big celebration and the changes Nugget had undergone. In fifteen minutes Fargo learned all there was to know; how a crotchety old prospector named Lester Wilkes had stumbled on a vein of rich ore after his donkey ran off and he followed it into a canyon. No sooner did Wilkes file a claim than a thousand more money-hungry souls swarmed into the area, and almost overnight the mining camp of Nugget had been born. Mines were established. Tools and lumber were freighted in and buildings sprang up one after the other. Now Nugget was thriving, with the promise of greater things to come.

"We owe it all to Mayor Quinby," the gabby player commented. "He's one clever cuss. His footrace has brought in folks from as far away as California, Salt Lake City, and points east."

"I heard tell Spike Yokum has laid ten to one odds his runner wins," another player mentioned, "and he wouldn't do that unless he has a sure thing going."

"Who's this Yokum?" Fargo casually inquired.

The gabby player snorted. "You must be new to these parts! Spike is only the biggest man in Nugget. What he says goes!"

"I thought Mayor Quinby ran things."

"He likes to think he does. Oh, sure, he's president of his own bank and heads up the chamber of commerce. But the real power is Spike Yokum. He has his fingers in every till in town. Every prospector, every miner, pays him a percentage of their take."

"Protection money? And the law allows it?"

Gabby cackled and smacked the table. "What's the law got to do with anything, sonny? When a gent is as mean and tough as Spike Yokum, with close to twenty gun hands at his beck and call, he can do whatever he wants."

"What about your marshal?"

"Tom Darnell? That drunk couldn't find his backside without a lamp and a map. He spends all his time holed up in his office nursing a bottle. When push comes to shove, he's about as worthless as a teat on a bull."

"I can't say as I blame him," another player said. "I sure wouldn't want to go up against the pack of killers Yokum imported. Why, any one of them would gun a man down for looking at him crosswise."

"The worst is that fella with the silver hair," Gabby commented. "The one who dresses all in black. It gives me goose bumps just being near him. And those eyes of his! They're enough to give a person nightmares!"

Fargo glanced up from his cards. "Silver hair? You wouldn't happen to know his handle, would you?"

"I know all their names," the gabby player bragged, and ticked them off on his fingers. "There's Mitch and Harley and Gannon. There's Clemmons and Little Tom and Arnold Scrim."

"Where have you been?" another piped up. "Scrim rode out a few days ago. Bound for Texas, the story goes."

"What about the one with the silver hair?" Fargo reminded them. Only one gunman he knew of answered that description, but he wanted to be sure.

"Him? Oh, he's known as—" Gabby abruptly stopped, his eyes widening. "Lord Almighty! What has those fellers so stirred up?"

Fargo snapped his head around.

The gunmen he had confronted were stalking into the saloon. Mitch and Harley had hunted him down, and they had brought friends along.

2

Skye Fargo calmly added four bits to the pot to stay in the game. The other players were riveted in growing dismay and fright as the gun sharks spread out. Mitch and Harley strode up to the table and glowered.

"Thought you'd seen the last of us, did you?" the straw-haired Harley demanded, his right hand inches from his revolver, his body as tense as barbed wire.

"You should have left town while you had the chance," Mitch exclaimed. "Now we're about to pay you back in spades."

"Are the eight of you enough?" Fargo pretended to be interested in his cards while watching the gunmen out of the corners of his eyes.

"Are you sayin' we can't take you ourselves?" Harley challenged. "That maybe we're not tough enough?"

"Out of the mouths of idiots," Fargo responded. He was playing with fire, trying to get them so mad that when he made his move, they would be a shade too slow. He couldn't drop all of them, that was for sure, but he would take as many with him as possible.

Mitch rubbed a welt on his temple. "Before we're done with you, you'll think you were stomped in a cattle stampede."

"Where have I heard that before?" Fargo dryly commented. The rest of the players were fidgeting in their chairs, dearly anxious to be anywhere other than where they were. He couldn't blame them. Innocent bystanders were routinely wounded or killed in saloon shoot-outs.

Harley was practically beside himself. "Get up, damn you, and take your medicine. Or so help me, I'll gun you where you sit."

Sighing, Fargo slowly laid down his cards. He knew that as soon as he pushed his chair back they would go for their hardware. So he tensed to flip backward instead, chair and all.

Then a strange thing happened.

The bat-wing doors creaked. Everyone in the saloon glanced toward them, and everyone in the saloon went a shade pale. Harley and Mitch were the worst of all, their fear as real as it was inexplicable.

With a bearish snarl a voice demanded, "What the hell is going on?"

Harley's mouth moved but no words came out, while Mitch averted his gaze. Their gun arms went limp.

The gabby player across the table licked his thin lips, then blurted, "Mr. Yokum, sir! How do you do? It's a pleasure to see you again."

"Shut up, Floyd."

"Yes, sir. Sorry, sir. You know me. I always aim to please." Floyd withered in his chair.

Boots scraped on the scuffed floor. Two men walked into Fargo's view. One was a bull buffalo in an expensive suit who radiated arrogance like the sun gave off light. It had to be Yokum. His shoulders were twice the size of most, his arms as thick as fence posts. He had a bullet head sprinkled with short red hair, a jaw like an anvil, and dark eyes that glittered like a wolverine's. He was the sort of man who could instill terror by his mere presence, and he knew it.

On his heels strutted a runt of a leather-slapper. Not five feet tall, he had prematurely silver hair but a face as smooth as a baby's backside. He was dressed entirely in black, which made the pearl grips on his

15

twin Smith and Wesson revolvers stand out all the more. His boots, gun belt and spurs showed Mexican influence, a hint he had at one time lived south of the border, or near it.

Spike Yokum raked the gunmen with eyes that lent the illusion they could bore through metal. "I haven't heard an explanation yet."

Harley glanced at Mitch but Mitch looked away. "It's nothin' much, boss." Harley forced a grin. "We were just fixin' to pay this stranger back, is all."

Yokum said nothing.

Harley continued, talking faster. "You see, we were aimin' to have some fun with these Apaches. You know, the ones who are here with Amarillo for the big race. But this bastard in buckskins about made a heifer out of me and pistol-whipped Mitch. So we decided to look him up." Harley stopped.

Spike Yokum had held up a hand with fingers as thick as tent pegs. "Refresh my memory, gentlemen. What were my orders about causing trouble while the celebration is under way?"

Harley's grin faded. "You wanted us to behave ourselves so as not to give the pilgrims a scare."

"Do you remember why?"

"It has something to do with money." Harley nervously wiped his hands on his pants.

"Nugget won't grow, won't prosper, if it acquires a reputation for lawlessness. We don't want potential investors scared off. We don't want decent folk afraid to move here. I want the town to grow, Harley. The bigger it becomes, the richer I become. I made that perfectly plain."

"Yes, yes, you did." Harley's chin bobbed. "And I'm right sorry for havin' a little too much tarantula juice and forgettin' what you said."

"Being sorry isn't enough. When I give an order I expect it to be obeyed." Spike Yokum glanced at the small man in black. "I'm afraid Silvermane, here, will have to dispose of you."

Fargo had heard that name before. Many times, in fact. In saloons and taverns from the Mississippi River to the Pacific Ocean. It was said Silvermane could throw lead with the best of them. That he was a shootist par excellence, an assassin who only hired out to the highest bidders. Forty men or more had fallen to his pearl-handled six-guns, or so the rumor mill had it.

Harley's terror was thick enough to cut with a dull butter knife. He backed up a few steps, mewing, "Now you just hold on! You can't go gunnin' a man down for a little thing like that!"

Silvermane's confidence was frightening in itself. "Tell me when and where, Mr. Yokum, and it's as good as done."

"Please!" Harley bawled at Spike Yokum. "Why pick on me? Mitch and Newton were on the prod, too."

"Consider this an object lesson. And quit sniveling. It's most unbecoming in an adult."

In a display of more intelligence than Fargo credited him with, Harley flung his arms over his head. "No! I refuse! Everyone is a witness. I'm not going for my gun. It would be murder."

Yokum's smile was a mask of viciousness. "You must consider yourself marvelously clever. But I advise you to be out of town within the hour or the consequences won't be to your liking."

"You don't have to tell me twice!" Harley scooted toward the entrance as if his pants were on fire.

The bat-wing doors had barely closed when Spike Yokum turned to Silvermane. "His horse is boarded at the North Street Stable. Follow him. A mile out should be sufficient. Leave the carcass for the vultures."

Silvermane nodded and ambled out.

"Now then," Yokum said, and stared hard at Fargo. "Suppose you tell me who you are and why you stood up for those Apaches?"

"Suppose I don't, and you go badger someone else." Fargo locked eyes with the larger man and for the span of half a minute a silent test of wills took place, a test that ended when Spike Yokum smiled thinly.

"Well, well. A wolf has come to town. You're not afraid. Not one bit. I admire that quality. Very few people are totally fearless. I've known only three in my lifetime. I'm one. My associate, Mr. Silvermane, is another. And now you." He held out a calloused hand. "Permit me to start over. I'm Theodore Yokum, but for reasons I won't go into, everyone refers to me as Spike. Who might you be?"

Fargo told him, and shook. The latent power in the other's grip was formidable. Yokum easily had to be one of the strongest individuals he had ever met.

"Why is it I have the feeling I've heard your name before?" The big man scratched his square chin, then shrugged. "Oh well. It will come to me eventually. In the meantime, I trust you will make the most of the pleasant diversions our fair town has to offer." He headed toward the doors, his gunmen in his wake. Pushing open a bat-wing, he glanced back. "You might stop at my establishment later. The Motherlode Saloon, four blocks south. I'll treat you to the first round."

For long moments after Yokum and his pack of killers had departed, the room was as still as a graveyard at midnight. Then Floyd let out a long breath and declared, "Mister, you must have oysters made of lead! No one has ever made Spike back down before."

"You'd best light a shuck," another advised. "Yokum ain't exactly the forgiving sort."

The last thing Fargo wanted was more trouble. By

the same token, he had his heart set on a night of liquor and lust. What should he do? he asked himself.

The answer came in the voluptuous shape of a dove in a tight green dress. She sashayed over, her hips saucily swaying, her bosom about ready to split the seams. A brunette, she wore her hair in a bun. Green eyes and cherry red lips added to her allure. Wreathed by tantalizing perfume, she rested a hand on his shoulder. "Say there, good-looking. You wouldn't happen to be in the mood for some company, would you?"

Fargo wrapped an arm around her slim waist and guided her down onto his knee. "You're in luck, gorgeous. That's just the mood I'm in." He lightly pecked her neck. "What time do you get off?"

"Not until midnight." She playfully rubbed the edge of his ear and pinched the lobe. "Marta Endelstrom is the name. Born and raised in good old Ohio. I came west with my husband, bound for the Promised Land, and the idiot went and got himself killed by hostiles."

Fargo divined the rest. Cast on hard times, with no money to her name and no one to turn to, she had done as hundreds of her sisters before her and accepted the only work she could find. "Is your boss here?"

"In the back. Why?"

"Fetch him." Fargo picked up his cards. "Now where were we?" It was several minutes before Marta came out of the back with a pinch-faced man in an apron.

"Marta says you wanted to see me. What about?"

"She needs to get off early. Ten o'clock, say." Fargo turned over his hand, a full house, and raked in the pot.

"And why should I do a damn fool thing like that? She's one of my best girls. Hooks the customers and keeps them drinking. Those two extra hours will cost me forty dollars or better in lost revenue."

Fargo fished in his shirt pocket, extracted his roll, and forked over forty. "This fair?"

The owner fondled the money as he would a lover. "I wish everyone was as reasonable." The bills disappeared under his apron. Patting Marta on the arm, he said, "If you want her off early, it's fine by me."

Beaming like the cat that had caught the canary, Marta roosted on Fargo's knee again. "You sure know how to impress a lady. The rest of the day I'm yours and yours alone."

Things were looking up. Fargo spent the next few hours engrossed in a battle of cards and wits. Between Marta and him, they polished off two-thirds of his bottle. When he announced he was calling it quits, he had recouped the forty, and ten extra.

"What now, handsome? I know a good restaurant if you're hungry. I don't eat there much because it's so pricey."

Fargo was hungry, although not for food. For now he would forego his craving. "Lead the way." He smacked her bottom.

Giggling, Marta linked her arm with his. "Something tells me this will be a night I'm not liable to forget."

As hot as it was inside, outside it was worse. A solid wall of heat slammed into them, bringing beads of sweat to Fargo's forehead within a few steps. Marta had snagged a pink parasol from behind the bar on their way out, and she opened it.

"I swear, if it gets any worse I'll be tempted to walk around naked."

They had the restaurant pretty much to themselves. It was well past midday but too early yet for the supper crowd. Fargo chose a corner table and sat with his back to the wall, a precaution he took out of habit. The waiter brought a pitcher of water, and he polished off a glass in quick gulps. As they were studying the menu a tiny bell over the door tinkled and in walked a familiar face.

Earl Desmond Sherwood had changed into an immaculate suit. With him was a stunning blonde whose features were as flawless as a priceless gem. The earl guided her toward a table at the front, then spotted Fargo, smiled broadly, and made for their table instead.

"I say! Fancy running into you again, old bean. Would it be presumptuous of me to ask to join you?"

Fargo's first inclination was to say no. But a closer look at the blonde changed his mind. She had lips as full and ripe as fresh plucked strawberries, and the way her dress clung to her thighs left nothing to the imagination. "Be my guest."

The earl slid out a chair for his companion, then sank down beside her. "Permit me to introduce Miss Penelope Ashton. She hails from Liverpool, the same as I. We've been friends since childhood. I love her like a sister."

Fargo could think of better ways to love her but refrained from saying so. He introduced Marta and himself.

"This is the gentleman I was telling you about earlier," Sherwood told Penelope. "The one who accosted us in the middle of our run."

The blonde's eyes lit with wry glee. "All to save a damsel in presumed distress, I understand. How gallant of you, Mr. Fargo. And how enlightening. I wasn't aware the colonists bred to such high standards."

"The colonists?" Fargo repeated.

Sherwood nodded. "Penelope, I'm afraid, is of the opinion America was better off as part of the British Empire. Like many of my countrymen, she regards you Americans as renegade colonials."

The blonde folded her hands. "I can speak in my own defense, Desmond. In my opinion, backwoods mentality has run riot here. Your country is overrun by louts and barbarians of every stripe."

Fargo was set to take her down a peg but Marta beat him to it.

"Listen to you, lady! A person would think you were the Queen herself, the airs you put on. But I daresay you step into your drawers one leg at a time like the rest of us."

Penelope Ashton sniffed as if she had caught a foul odor. "How crude. But I should expect no less from a provincial who wears apparel better suited to a waterfront dive than polite society."

"I'll show you polite," Marta declared, and started to rise, but a restraining hand from Fargo held her in her seat.

"Ladies, if you please." The earl wagged a finger at each of them, then focused on Ashton. "Penelope, I must insist you stop treating everyone here like you do your servants. Had I known you would behave so abominably, I'd never have brought you along."

"I'm sorry, Desmond, but I don't share your quaint affection for backwards cultures. I mean, really. Most of the women I've seen wear the plainest of clothes and make no attempt to beautify themselves. And the men are either shy simpletons who treat me as if I'm made of glass, or randy goats who have the nerve to undress me with their eyes as if I'm a common strumpet."

"Those women you mentioned," Fargo spoke up, "can't afford more than one or two dresses a year. Any extra money they have goes to their families, not for war paint. And those simpletons are men who were brought up to believe they should treat women with respect."

"Imagine that," Marta snipped. "Barbarians with manners."

Penelope flushed scarlet, and for a few moments Fargo thought the two women would tear into each other. Thankfully, Sherwood quickly, and wisely, changed the subject.

"I say, this promises to be a grand race! Competitors from all over have come. Luther Samuels, for instance, is from North Carolina. There's a gentleman from New York, another from Virginia. Of course, no one has traveled quite as far as I have."

"You came all the way from England just for this?" Fargo said to keep the conversation flowing.

"I should say not. I was in Denver several weeks ago, on a tour of your West, when I saw an advertisement in the Denver press. Mayor Quinby, I understand, placed them in newspapers all over, well in advance." Desmond smiled. "I simply couldn't resist."

"Like to run, do you?" Fargo tried to catch the waiter's attention so they could order.

"It would be more apt to say I love to run. It's been in my blood since I was a youngster. I've participated in dozens of races in half as many countries. Not for the prize money, you understand. For the sheer thrill of the competition." There was no denying the earl's sincerity.

Fargo didn't share the Englishman's enthusiasm. He ran when he had to, and that was it. Otherwise, he preferred horseback. "You're up against a lot of other runners," he noted.

"Yes. Five dozen, possibly." Sherwood excitedly rubbed his hands together. "Which is fine by me! The greater the challenge, the sweeter the triumph."

"Getting ahead of yourself, aren't you?"

"Not really. Few of the other runners have my experience. That Indian girl, Swift Fox, is a competent bit of goods. She promises to keep me on my toes. But I'm a professional and she's not. The only other runner in my class is Richard Thorne. He hasn't arrived yet but they expect him by tomorrow morning." Casually, as if it were of no importance, the earl commented, "I expect he'll be the local favorite, what with Mr. Yokum backing him."

Fargo temporarily forgot about the waiter. "Yokum has his own runner? What do you know about him?"

"Richard and I have competed against one another

before. He's fast, he is, and he can run for hours without tiring. There was a time when he took his running seriously. Now he hires his legs out to whoever can afford his high fee."

The race, Fargo reflected, was shaping up to be extremely interesting. He might stick around just to see who won. "What about Amarillo?"

Sherwood sat back. "He's an unknown quantity, that one. He never speaks. Never gives a clue to what is going on in his head. But as the Lord is my witness, that Apache can run with the best of them. On all our practice runs, he's always near the head of the pack." Sherwood tapped the table, pensive. "I suspect he's been holding back and never showing us what he's really capable of."

That would be just like an Apache, Fargo nearly said out loud. Secretive by nature as well as training, they regarded every non-Apache as a potential enemy. 'Trust no one' was their way of life, ingrained by teaching and temperament. It was why Apaches never revealed their Apache names for fear of giving someone power over them. In all their dealings with outsiders, they used Spanish names. "Is there anyone else you think has a chance of winning?"

"Precious few, I'm afraid. Most of the contestants are locals who are eighty pence to the pound. Store clerks, stable boys and prospectors who have no idea what they're in for." Sherwood gazed at shafts of sunlight streaming through the front window. "It's a ten mile course over some of the most rugged terrain I've ever seen. The heat alone will cause three-fourths to drop out before they've gone more than a few miles."

Penelope Ashton surprised Fargo by smiling and urging, "So tell us, my buckskin prince. Who will you lay your money on?"

Fargo would almost swear she had stressed the word "lay." Deciding it must be wishful thinking on his part, he answered, "I generally confine my gambling to the poker table." Although he had on occasion bet on a horse race or three.

"Ah. I do so like cards but I've never had the pleasure of learning poker. Perhaps you would be so kind as to teach me sometime?"

Again, Fargo was sure she had accented "pleasure." He glanced at the earl but Sherwood hadn't noticed. Or maybe he had and it was of no consequence to him.

Marta quirked her luscious mouth. "Maybe you should teach her strip poker, Skye. If it's not too barbaric for her."

Just then the waiter finally appeared, nipping their verbal war in the bud. Fargo ordered a steak and "enough coffee to drown a horse." It occurred to him he had left his whiskey bottle at the saloon but it was too late to go back. By now someone else had polished off what little was left.

While they waited, the earl made small talk about how life in England differed from life in America. "The one thing I can never get used to is your fondness for firearms. In my country it's illegal to walk around with a pistol strapped around your waist."

"In your country you don't have hostiles out to count coup by lifting your scalp. Or outlaws who will fill you with lead to steal a few measly dollars. Or bears that can rip you to ribbons with one blow." Fargo could go on but he didn't bother. He pushed his hat back and noticed Penelope studying him on the sly.

Marta also noticed. "Tell me, dearie. Would you say the men on this side of the pond are as handsome as those on your side?"

"As a lady I don't interest myself in such trivial matters."

"As a lady, I'd say you were full of—" Marta began, but left her statement unfinished when Fargo shook his head.

An awkward silence descended. When their meals arrived, Fargo ate like one half starved. He was down to his last piece of succulent meat when the front door opened and in barreled Spike Yokum and two gunmen. Instinctively, he tensed and lowered his right hand to his lap. He had a hunch it wasn't a coincidence and Yokum proved him right by striding directly toward them.

"What's this, then?" Sherwood whispered.

Yokum nodded at each of the ladies, then declared, "Mr. Fargo! I've been giving it some thought and I've decided I was too hasty a while ago. You and I need to a talk."

"About what?"

"About you coming to work for me." Yokum leaned on the table. "And keep in mind I never take no for an answer."

3

Skye Fargo liked to think he was a shrewd judge of character, but Spike Yokum puzzled him. The man had the look of a saloon tough but he dressed and talked like a banker. Yokum was also unpredictable, as he demonstrated by ordering the death of one of his own men. To have him march into the restaurant like this was the last thing Fargo expected.

Yokum had turned to the Englishman. "I understand Richard Thorne has competed against you before. He wrote me that you're the only one who has a prayer of beating him."

"Flattering, sir, but not entirely true," the earl replied. "As I was explaining to Mr. Fargo before you came in, there are several others who shouldn't be taken lightly. The Crow woman. Mr. Samuels. That Apache fellow. They're all superior competitors."

"That's nice to know." Yokum shifted back to Fargo. "Let's get right to it. I'm a busy man and I don't like beating around the bush. I need to find someone to replace Mr. Harley, and I believe you're just the one for the job."

"Do you always hire people you know nothing about?"

"To the contrary. A short while ago it hit me where I had heard your name before." Yokum studied Fargo closely. "You're the one they write about in the newspapers and the penny dreadfuls. The scout who can

27

track an ant across solid rock, the plainsman who never loses his way, the marksman who can drop a buffalo at a thousand yards."

"Those stories are exaggerated." Fargo wasn't responsible for the tall tales printed about him. Few had any basis in fact, and those that did were so distorted as to qualify as flights of fiction. Truth was, they were more grief than they were worth.

"In every lie there is a kernel of truth," Yokum responded. "I suspect you are much too modest. In either event, a man like you would be invaluable. And I'm willing to pay top dollar for your services."

"I'm not looking for work."

"Not even for five hundred dollars a month?"

Fargo heard Marta whistle softly. That was more than most people earned in a year. More than the army ever paid for his services, more than he could earn as a tracker or guide.

"You need not answer right now. Sleep on it and look me up in the morning." Yokum was on his way out. "I'll be at the Motherlode from eight until ten."

Popping the last morsel of steak into his mouth, Fargo watched Nugget's pillar of power hustle down the street.

"I say, you've made quite the impression," Sherwood complimented him. "I don't see how you can refuse. Mr. Yokum strikes me as the sort who always gets what he's after."

Yokum struck Fargo as the kind he could never turn his back on. Not unless he wanted a slug between the shoulders. "Let's head back," he said to Marta.

Sherwood politely rose. "I hope we meet again soon. Perhaps you would let me treat you to a sherry."

"Make it a bottle of coffin varnish and you have a deal."

Fargo and Marta had gone a block and a half when the short hairs at the nape of his neck prickled. He checked but saw no one following them. The feeling persisted, and by the time they reached the saloon where she worked, he had a crick in his neck from glancing back so often.

Business had picked up. Fargo treated himself to a second bottle of red-eye and sat in on a poker game. His cards were red hot. Marta on his knee, he was content to play the rest of the afternoon away. By six that evening the place was jammed.

A player tapped out and excused himself. Into his chair sank another familiar face, crowned by a floppy brown hat.

"If it ain't the good Samaritan," Luther Samuels commented. "Helped any old ladies across the street lately? Or maybe saved a kitten up a tree?"

"Ever heard of letting something lie?" Fargo replied.

"Hogwash like that is for weaklings who ain't got the gumption to take what they want from life." Samuels set a poke on the table, opened it, and fished out some coins.

"And you do?"

Samuels looked up. "Damn right! I was born a slave, but you don't see me pickin' cotton, do you? No siree. And you know why? Because I struck out on my own to live as I see fit."

A townsman impatiently drummed his fingers. "Are we here to play cards or listen to you brag on yourself?"

"You're here to lose money to me," Samuels smirked. "I have to get me a lot of cash, fast. That's why I'm going to win the footrace. Because I need that ten thousand more than anyone else. Need it so much I can taste it."

The townsman wasn't impressed. "Sounds like you're putting the cart before the horse. I'm betting on that Crow gal. They say she won three races last year, two the year before."

An elderly player had his own opinion. "The Englishman has won quite a few, too, and he's been at it longer than anyone else. I think he'll outlast the whole bunch."

"Are you loco?" someone asked. "England is cold and rainy all the time. He's not used to one hundred and five degree heat. That Apache, on the other hand, is. I say he'll come out on top."

Luther Samuels was staring at Fargo. "How about you, do-gooder? Who do you pick?"

"I don't much care."

"Do the smart thing, then. Place your money on me. It's a sure thing."

One of the townsmen expressed Fargo's own sentiments by saying, "Hell, friend. Nothing in this world is a sure thing. The best we can hope for is to make it to the grave in one piece."

The cards were dealt, and everyone clammed up. Fargo played cautiously, unwilling to lose his stake. Samuels, however, was positively reckless. He bet high on hands that weren't worth it and bluffed when he shouldn't. Small wonder, an hour later, that he slammed his hand on the table, scooped up the few coins he had left, and stood. "Count me out."

The townsman chuckled. "If you run like you play cards, you'll be lucky to finish last."

"Is that so?" Furious, Samuels lunged across the table. He seized the man by the shirt, hoisted him up, and shoved.

The townsman squawked in fright as he toppled but he came up mad as a wet cat. "You damned darkie! You had no call to do that." A derringer streaked from under his right sleeve.

Everyone froze, Luther Samuels included.

"Don't ever lay a hand on me again." The townsman couldn't seem to decide whether he was going to shoot or not.

As luck would have it, out of the crowd stepped a mousey man in a high-crowned hat and a well-worn vest to which a battered tin star had been pinned.

"That'll be enough, Ed. Put that peashooter of yours away before you hurt yourself." He pointed at Samuels. "As for you, I saw the whole thing. You'd better go cool off before I throw you behind bars and keep you there until after the race."

The townsman obeyed, muttering, "Sure thing, Marshal Darnell."

Not Samuels. As usual, he was too pigheaded for his own good. "You'll let him go but put *me* in jail? Don't like blacks, is that it? There's nothing I hate more than a bigot with a badge."

Darnell sighed. He had perpetually sad eyes and a matching perpetual frown. "There's nothing I hate more than a moron with a chip on his shoulder. It wouldn't matter to me if you were black, orange or purple. Make yourself scarce or do time."

Based on what Fargo had been told, he half expected the lawman to be an alcoholic ruin. But although Samuels cursed up a storm, Darnell didn't back down, and after a few seconds he pounded on the table and stormed out, pushing people right and left.

"He must be a wizard at making friends," Tom Darnell remarked. He turned to go, then noticed Fargo. "I take it you're the famous scout I've heard so much about? You certainly match the description I was given." He offered his hand. "I've been looking forward to meeting you."

"Why would that be?"

"I thought maybe the two of us could share a drink. My treat." The lawman motioned toward the bar. "I won't take much of your time. I promise. But it's important."

"Save my seat," Fargo instructed Marta, and followed the lawman over.

"My usual apple cider," Darnell told the barkeep.

Fargo turned and leaned against the counter. "Cider? Word has it you're fond of harder stuff."

"A drunk, is more like it. But even someone who likes sucking down the tarantula juice as much as I do has to sober up now and then. Not by choice, mind you. I'm under orders to stay clean until after the race."

"From Mayor Quinby or Spike Yokum?"

"Both. For once they're in agreement. They want I should present a positive image, as the good mayor described it, for the town's sake." Darnell accepted his drink and sipped. "Shrewd of you to peg the reason. Especially for someone who has only been in town a short while."

"I keep my eyes and ears open."

"So do I, believe it or not. And the wind has whispered in my ear that Spike Yokum offered you a job." Marshal Darnell scanned those around them, then said quietly, "A word to the wise. Don't take it."

Fargo regarded the lawman a moment. "What would Yokum say if he found out you were bucking him?"

"Most likely he would have me strung up by my thumbs and bullwhipped. He doesn't like being crossed. It's one of his many flaws. So I'm counting on you not to spill the beans."

"Why this interest in my welfare?"

"I don't want another death on my conscience." Darnell swirled the remaining cider in the glass. "Anyone who gets Yokum mad has a habit of disappearing without a trace. Eleven so far that I know of, and I have suspicions about a dozen more."

Fargo's whiskey arrived but he didn't touch it just yet. "Anything else on your mind?"

"I overheard some of Yokum's men. They thought I was passed out over my desk but I was shamming." Darnell's voice dropped until it was barely more than a whisper. "The job offer is a ruse. Yokum wants to keep you close until after the race, when he'll deal with you in a more permanent nature."

"Is that so?" To Fargo it still made no sense.

"Would I be here if it weren't? Yokum was fit to bust a gut when you backed down his boys in public. Worse, he had to have one of his top lieutenants killed to show what happens to those who disobey him. Now he plans to even the score."

"I'm obliged for the warning."

"You're welcome. If I were you, I'd head for parts unknown and leave Yokum to stew in his own bile. It would serve him right." Darnell gulped the rest of his drink. "I can't stay much longer. Someone might tell Yokum we were jawing and he might wonder what it was about."

"One last question. If push comes to shove, whose side are you on? Spike Yokum's? Or the mayor's?"

Marshal Darnell was quiet a bit. "What I do depends on whether or not I'm sober. At the moment I'm putting the town's welfare before everything else. But with a bottle or two in me—" He shrugged.

Fargo admired the man's honesty.

"One last thing. I ran into that English fellow, Sherwood, a while ago. He gave me the impression the two of you are on friendly terms. If that's the case, you might want to tell him to be on his guard."

"Why?"

"Spike Yokum never played fair in his life. I have no proof, mind you, but those men I overheard made a few comments that have me thinking it might be unhealthy to be one of the better runners."

The lawman left, leaving Fargo with a lot to think about. He sat back in on the card game and played until half past eight. Marta hovered over him like a hummingbird over sugar water; massaging his shoulders, rubbing his neck, and refilling his glass the moment it was empty. She stepped back when he suddenly stood and announced, "Thanks for the game, gents."

"I thought we weren't leaving until ten?" Marta mentioned.

"I have an errand to run. When I get back we'll head to your place. Enjoy another bottle on me until then." Fargo handed her enough money.

"I don't much like twiddling my thumbs but I guess I don't have any choice. Hurry back, big man, you hear?"

The cool night air was a welcome change. Fargo drank it in as he bent his steps toward the Carson Hotel. The earl was staying there with Penelope. Desmond had also mentioned they were going to attend a revival of *Nimrod Wildfire* at the new Nugget Theater, and invited Fargo and Marta to go along. Fargo had declined. He wasn't much for plays and opera and the like. Most of the actors and actresses he'd met in his travels had been so in love with themselves, it was a wonder they could tear themselves away from their mirrors.

Nimrod Wildfire wasn't due to end until eleven. Plenty of time for Fargo to leave a message at the hotel. Something short and to the point. Maybe 'Watch your back' would suffice.

Fargo went around a corner and quickly flattened against the building. Hidden in deep shadow, he waited. That prickling at the nape of his neck had returned, the feeling that had saved his hide more times than he could count.

Although the hour was late, Nugget's nightlife was still in full swing, and the street was abuzz with activity. Nearby strolled a painted lady parading her wares. A young thing in a dress two sizes too small, she bestowed an inviting look on every man who passed. Fargo saw her gaze down the street, smile seductively, and arch her back so her bosom was pointed at the stars.

"Hey there, gents. Can I interest you in an hour of more excitement than either of you have ever had?"

A pair of gunmen ambled into view. Both had been with Harley and Mitch at the saloon. One had a sloping brow and the stubble on his chin could be used to sand wood. The other was a lot younger, and her invite interested him.

"Get lost, you little tramp." Stubble-chin dashed the other's hopes. "We've got work to do."

"No need to be a horse's ass about it." The dove held her own. "If you don't want my company, fine."

"I wouldn't mind some," the younger gunman volunteered.

Stubble-chin shot him a barbed look. "I'll be sure and tell that to the boss if he asks where you got to."

Distracted by the dove, they walked past Fargo without realizing he was there. He stepped from the shadows. "You can tell him something for me, too."

Both gunmen spun. The younger started to lower his hand to his six-shooter but stubble-chin swatted his arm. "Don't be hasty, kid. Let me handle this." The older man adopted a crafty expression. "Who the blazes are you, mister? And why in hell did you jump out at us like that?"

"As if you don't know." Fargo was hoping one or the other would take a swing or try to draw. "I'll only say this once. Stop following me."

It was always the young ones who had mouths as wide as the Grand Canyon and brains as big as pebbles. "I don't take kindly to threats. My pard and I are out for a night on the town, minding our own business." He shoved Fargo's shoulder. "You'd be smart to do the same."

Fargo compromised. He slugged the kid in the gut, then kneed him in the face. Instantly, he rotated toward the other gunman but stubble-chin shook his head and backed up a few paces.

"Not me. No sir. I'm not that stupid."

"Let Yokum know that if he pulls this stunt again, I'm coming after him."

"If I admit to knowing him and he found out, he'd have me dance a strangulation jig as another of his object lessons." Stubble-chin glanced down at his partner, who was clutching a bloody nose and whining like a kicked puppy. "I'd say what you just did to Timmy here was message enough."

"Good. Pick him up and make yourselves scarce."

The Carson Hotel was one of the finest Nugget had to offer. It turned out to be catty-corner from the new theater. Lively music wafted into the night, punctuated by hearty applause. Fargo was directly across from the ornate entrance when a bronze gilded door was shoved wide open and out hustled none other than Earl Desmond Sherwood and his female friend, Penelope Ashton. They were leaving the show early.

Pleased by his stroke of luck, Fargo was about to shout to them when the door was pushed open again and out charged three roughhewn characters. They weren't wearing hog legs but each pulled a short wooden club from under his jacket or coat and converged.

The trio were on Sherwood in a twinkling. Shoving Penelope behind him, the earl confronted them. He twisted the stag head of his cane and suddenly a rapier-thin sword lanced in a practiced thrust. Its target yipped as it pierced the man's shoulder.

Another attacker caught Sherwood on the back with a blow powerful enough to spin him half around.

Fargo didn't announce his presence or warn the buzzards to stop. Undetected, he dashed over to the nearest, tore the club from the man's grasp, and when the startled assailant turned, smashed him in the face. A cheek crunched, and the man imitated a poled ox.

The other two were raining blows at Sherwood's legs, but so far the Englishman had adeptly held them at bay.

"Drop that pigsticker or it'll get worse for you!" the one who had been stabbed in the shoulder roared.

Fargo brought his club crashing down on the back of the man's skull. The last one heard the thud, and spun. Straight into the blow Fargo had swung at his ear. Again there was the crunch of bone. Again a limp figure sprawled to the ground.

Many of the passersby had stopped in their tracks, overcome by horror. Soon a crowd would gather.

Fargo threw the club down, grabbed the earl and the blonde by their elbows, and forcefully steered them toward the Carson Hotel. "Good thing I came by when I did."

"I'll say!" Sherwood declared. He was red-faced from his exertion but otherwise little the worse for wear. "Those bounders were following us around all evening, trying not to be obvious about it and failing abysmally. They were as subtle as elephants. When we saw them slinking toward our booth in the theater, I decided to get Penelope to safety. Footpads, I suspect, out to filch my money."

"Leg breakers, is more like it."

"I beg your pardon?"

"We'll talk inside." They reached the hotel lobby and found a plush sofa and matching chair over in a corner. Fargo let them sit but he remained standing so he could unlimber the Colt swiftly if need be. "Spike Yokum hired those men to break your legs so you can't take part in the race."

Sherwood was sliding the sword blade down into the cane. "I say! You know this for an indisputable fact?"

"I know that if you're not careful between now and race time, you'll be going back to England on crutches."

"Surely they wouldn't!"

Penelope Ashton had been strangely quiet. Out in the street she hadn't shown any fear or broken out in hysterics. To the contrary. She was calmness personified. "Honestly, Desmond. Get your head out of the sand. These people are uncouth louts. What else should you expect?"

"I've raced in America before, my dear, and the

events were always conducted aboveboard." Desmond twisted the gold-plated stag until there was a sharp *click*. "Say what you will, Americans are basically honest at heart."

Penelope sadly shook her beautiful head. "You're too trusting, Des. One day that flaw will be the death of you." She reached over and placed a hand on Fargo's knee. "I thank you for saving him from his naivete."

This time there was no mistake. Fargo felt her give a slight squeeze before she pulled her hand away.

The earl was offended. "I'm quite capable of taking care of myself, I'll have you know. I have half a mind to seek out Mayor Quinby and lodge a formal protest. Yokum should be brought up on charges."

"You'd need proof he was behind it, and those men aren't hankering to be worm food."

"Yokum would have them murdered to keep them quiet?" Sherwood was appalled.

Fargo realized Penelope Ashton was right. "Get this through your head. Spike Yokum will kill anyone who crosses him. The only reason he didn't have you shot was because Quinby and Nugget's decent citizens would raise a fuss."

"So he paid those bounders to break a few of my bones?" Sherwood was aghast. "I've never heard of anyone so unbelievably evil." He pursed his lips. "Are the rest of the competitors in any danger?"

"Only those who have any chance of winning, and they need to be warned."

"I'll do so tomorrow morning. We're having our last practice run." Desmond slid forward on the seat. "You've given me a lot to reflect on between now and then." He rose. "I might as well turn in. Coming, my dear?"

"You go ahead, Des. I'm not tired yet." Penelope said nothing else until the earl had gone up the stairs. Then she leaned over and placed her warm hand on

Fargo's knee. "How about you, Yank? Are you tired?"

"What did you have in mind?" Fargo bluntly asked.

"Escort me to my room and I'll show you."

4

Skye Fargo liked women as much as the next man. He rarely hesitated when a willing beauty invited him to treat himself to her charms. But this time he did. Something didn't quite add up. "I thought you disliked Americans. To you I'm just another uncouth barbarian," he quoted her.

Penelope Ashton's eyes danced with brazen delight. "How do I phrase this delicately? Barbarians have their merits. A lack of inhibitions is one of them. Most men on my side of the pond are much too stuffy."

"What about the earl?"

"What about him? Desmond and I are close friends, nothing more. We've never been intimate, if that's what you're hinting." Penelope ran the tip of her tongue along her luscious lips. "He's always the proper gentleman, and all that rubbish. But I'd wager you don't share his outlook."

Fargo experienced a stirring in his groin. Her shimmering blond hair, her full, buxom figure, the sensuous outline of her legs under her dress, were enough to arouse anyone.

"This is a one-time invitation," Penelope informed him. "I wouldn't take too long making up your mind or I'll be insulted."

Fargo thought of Marta. She was waiting for him

back at the saloon. But it was a good hour yet until ten o'clock, when he was to take her home.

Penelope slowly rose, her dress rustling. "What will it be? The pleasure of my company for a while? Or will you spend the rest of your life wondering what you missed?"

"Lead the way."

Her room was on the second floor, down the hall from the earl. "I didn't want one next to Des. He's a dear, but he tends to be too protective and has spoiled my fun on more than one occasion." Inserting her key, Penelope stroked Fargo's chin. "And I wouldn't want him spoiling things for us."

The furnishings were regal by frontier standards, including crystal lamps and mahogany furniture. But as the Englishwoman pulled the shade, she commented, "I'd ask you to forgive the crude accommodations but you must be accustomed to them."

Fargo bolted the door. When he turned, Penelope was sizing him up. Her gaze lingered below his gunbelt.

"That pompous twit, Mayor Quinby, told us that you are known as something of a ladies' man. I do so hope the claim isn't exaggerated."

"There's one way to find out." Walking over, Fargo wrapped an arm around her hips and pulled her close. He molded his mouth to hers and she parted her lips to admit his tongue. When, after a while, he broke the kiss, her smirk widened.

"Nice, but not heart stopping. Frankly, I expected better. And don't be so gentle. I prefer it rough."

Fargo cupped her bottom and squeezed none-too-gently. She squirmed, gave a slight "Oh!" and nipped his neck. He slid his right hand higher, up under her arm to her bosom. At the first contact she shivered deliciously. Again he squeezed, hard, and she cooed softly deep in her throat. Smothering the cry with his mouth, he inhaled her velvety tongue. This time when he pulled back her eyelids were hooded.

"Nice. Extremely nice. I trust it's a prelude of what's to come?"

Fargo kissed her smooth chin, her soft cheek. He sucked on her lower lip, which tasted like a fresh strawberry, then lightly bit it.

Gasping, Penelope drew away. But she wasn't mad. Far from it. "Now you're showing some spunk."

Abruptly placing both hands on her breasts, Fargo clamped his fingers tight. Most women would have yelped in pain. Not Penelope Ashton. Snapping her head back, she shuddered and gasped.

"Yesssssssss! That's how I like it!"

Scooping her into his arms, Fargo dumped her onto the bed. She lay in a wanton sprawl, her hair disheveled, her chest rising and falling, one leg crooked at the knee, affording him a glimpse of smooth inner thigh. His manhood surged. Tossing his hat onto a dresser, he unbuckled his gunbelt and dropped it onto the floor.

Penelope wriggled her hips. "Don't just stand there, luv. I'm not getting any younger."

Easing down beside her, Fargo pried at a row of tiny buttons on her European-style jacket. Thirty or more, he bet. He had unfastened about ten, nuzzling Penelope's neck all the while, when she impatiently pushed at his shoulders.

"What on earth is taking you so long? You're bumbling about like a bloody simpleton. Let me do it or we'll be here for a week."

"Is that so?" Gripping the front of the jacket in both hands, Fargo grinned. "I hope you know how to sew."

"You wouldn't dare! Have you any idea how much this cost? I bought it in Paris just for this trip."

Fargo bunched his muscles and wrenched. Buttons went flying every which way. He started to bend to kiss her and was jarred by a stinging slap to his left cheek.

"You insufferable clod! Didn't you hear me?" Penelope drew back her hand to slap him a second time.

Seizing her wrist, Fargo repaid the favor. He didn't hit her hard. Certainly nowhere near as hard as she had hit him. He figured it would make her madder but he was tired of her uppity airs.

Instead, Penelope laughed. "Ohhh. I liked that! Smack me a few more times, why don't you? Harder next time."

"You like pain, is that it?"

Nodding, Penelope kissed his jaw, his neck, his ear. Between kisses she said, "When I make love, I like to feel alive. To have the blood rushing in my veins. To have all my senses expanded." She bit him again. "It adds a little zest, don't you think?"

No, Fargo didn't. "If that's what you want, after we're done you can pound your head against the wall." He began undressing her, removing clothes as fast as he could, but it wasn't fast enough. Her nails dug into the back of his neck deep enough to draw drops of blood, then she reached under his shirt to rake his back.

"Hurry it up, you damnable tortoise!" Penelope taunted.

Fargo had put up with enough. He tore at her lacy underthings, shredding them like so much paper. The more he ripped, the more she laughed. Within half a minute her clothes were in tatters and he reared up on his knees, his skin as hot as a skillet, his breathing uneven.

Penelope's tousled hair fanned across the pillow. Rigid nipples, as inviting as drops of honey, crowned creamy breasts as superb as any Fargo ever saw. Strips of cloth were draped across them like bright ribbons on a gift. Her stomach was flat, her thatch a golden down. She had thighs that went on forever and calves most women would die for. She was, in short, exquisite. "Like what you see, big man?"

Fargo liked it a lot. Removing his shirt, he tossed it to the floor, then tugged off his boots and pants. He had to admit her silly antics had him excited. Swooping his mouth to her right breast, he flicked the nipple with his tongue, then lightly nipped it.

"Ah! More!"

Penelope might be a lady but she had the same carnal passions as every other female. Her hands were all over him, exploring, molding, caressing. Her molten mouth covered every square inch between his shoulders and his brow. The moist tip of her tongue rimmed his ear.

Fargo felt her fingers close on his iron manhood, shattering his focus. He gasped as she slowly slid her fingers up and down. Only by sheer force of will did he keep from exploding too soon. Mentally pulling himself back from the brink, he switched his mouth to her other breast, then lathered the cleavage between them.

Penelope cupped him, low down, and a constriction formed deep in Fargo's throat. Placing a thumb and a forefinger on her right nipple, he pinched it and was rewarded with a yelp. Not a yelp of pain, but a yelp of pure, unadulterated pleasure.

"Harder, luv! Hurt me!"

Any harder and Fargo would tear her nipple off. But he pinched the other one, just the same, and she sank her teeth into his collar bone. He glided his hand over her downy thatch to the junction of her milky thighs. She was moist to the touch and shivered when he parted her nether lips. Penelope groaned when he flicked her swollen knob and cried out softly when he inserted his finger clear to the knuckle.

"Ohhhhhh. You're starting to get to me!"

Fargo inserted a second finger, and wriggled them. It brought her tight bottom up off the bed and elicited another low cry. She glued her mouth to his, greedily devouring his lips and tongue. Her every breath was molten, her body a finely tuned guitar desirous of being strummed.

Penelope shifted her hands to his backside. Her nails sheared into his skin and she clawed at him like an alley cat in heat. "Scratch me, too," she mewed. "Cut me. Beat me. Whatever you want."

What Fargo wanted was for her to quit begging to be hurt and simply take it as it came. Had he known how fond she was of pain, he might not have taken her up on her offer. Or was he kidding himself? After all, when it came to women, "no" wasn't an answer he heard himself giving all that much.

"What are you waiting for? An engraved invitation from the Queen?"

Fargo pressed his member to her womanhood. Inch by inch he slid all the way in, filling her. For most women that was enough. But not Penelope Ashton.

"Hit me! Anywhere! Everywhere! I want you to thrash me or I won't enjoy it as much."

"I left my whip and chains in my saddlebags," Fargo quipped. He had her by the hips, and now he commenced to thrust his engorged member into her wet tunnel. She met each one with matching ardor but he had the impression her body was responding on its own, that she had drawn back emotionally.

"You sure know how to ruin a girl's fun," Penelope complained. Her face hardened. "Bloody hell! If that's how you want to play this, then that's the way it will be."

Fargo felt her legs slide up over his and her ankles lock behind his back. He wasn't quite sure what she was up to until she slammed herself against him like a flesh-and-blood battering ram. A sly smile spread across her features and she did it again, arching her spine until she resembled a bow.

"Some people just don't listen," Fargo growled, and did some ramming of his own.

A gleam entered Penelope's eyes, a gleam that had nothing to do with their lovemaking and everything to do with her state of mind. She drove herself at him in ever-increasing abandon, demonstrating surprising strength, her nails fixed into his upper arms.

Clenching his teeth, Fargo gave as good as he got. Their coupling became a battle of wills, a test to determine which one exploded first, and he would be damned if it was going to be him.

"Yes! Yes! Harder!" Penelope urged.

Fargo slammed into her and she threw herself right back at him. He gripped her heaving breasts and squeezed hard enough to burst real melons.

"Ah! Like thaaaaaaattt!"

The bed sounded as if it were on the verge of breaking apart. The legs were smacking the floorboards like hammers, the mattress close to buckling. Fargo had never made such violent love in his life, and, Lord help him, he was as caught up in it as she was. He relished every stroke of his pole, every quiver of her sheath. Their bodies vibrated with raw lust.

For her part, Penelope wheezed like a bellows, her lustrous skin slick with perspiration, the hint of a smile curling her scarlet lips. Her eyelids fluttered and her nails dug in deeper. "More!" she beseeched him. "Give me more!"

Fargo knees were hurting and his thigh muscles ached but he wouldn't stop for anything short of the end of the world. Over and over he drove up into her. Over and over he lifted her off the quilt. The occupants of neighboring rooms were bound to hear but he didn't care.

Suddenly Penelope reared up and bit him on the chest, ripping into him as he might rip into jerky. Fleeting pain lanced through his body. He was aware of her fists striking his shoulders, his face. She was loco, this prim and proper Englishwoman. Stark, raving crazy when it came to lovemaking But there was a method to her violence.

"I'm there!" Penelope suddenly cried. Her lovely eyes widened, her flawless mouth parted. She gushed, a physical and emotional release the likes of which Fargo had seldom witnessed. Thrashing, kicking, screaming, she came repeatedly, her inner walls wrapped tight around his pulsing manhood. For minutes it went on. Then her movements slowed and she coasted from the heights.

Fargo could hear the thunderous beat of his own heart. His mouth went dry, his skin tingled. He almost cried out himself when the moment came. Throwing back his head, he opened his mouth but all that escaped his throat was a guttural growl. Then came the pleasure, in wave after blissful wave. The room swam and danced.

Fargo always wished moments like this could last forever, but they never did. All too soon he crested the peak and floated toward earth. His senses still reeled and his blood still hammered, but ever slower. Uttering a groan, he collapsed on top of her, his chest cushioned by hers.

Penelope went completely limp. Eyes shut, she drew in long, deep breaths, and let them out through her nose. Her knees were bent wide, her inner thighs drenched. "Not bad," she whispered.

Easing onto his left shoulder, Fargo winced. It felt like he had just been mauled by a pack of wolves. Or gone ten rounds in the ring. Everything ached; his head, his shoulders, his chest, his back. He was bleeding in three or four spots. His scalp hurt where she had nearly pulled a handful of hair out by the roots. He tasted blood in his mouth and discovered she had cut his lower lip. "Damn."

"Something wrong, lover?"

"Next time you want a tumble in the sack, find yourself a grizzly."

Penelope's finger rimmed his battered ear. "Poor baby. Did I hurt you? Did I wear out the big, strapping frontiersman?" Grinning, she rolled onto her side with her back to him. "How the colonies ever beat us, I will never understand."

The temptation was too much for Fargo to resist. He brought his right hand down, palm open, with a sharp *smack* that sounded like the crack of a bullwhip. Penelope yelped and came up off the bed as if he had scorched her with hot coals.

"Hey! That hurt!"

Fargo touched his lower lip. "Tell me about it." Secretly, it gratified him to see the bright red handprint on her pert buttock. "You're the one who likes pain, remember?"

Penelope rubbed her bottom. "Don't fret. The black and blue marks will go away in a few days, the cuts will heal, and you'll be good as new."

Fargo was more concerned about what Marta would say. Some women were sensitive about being with a man who had just been with another woman. But it wasn't as if they were married or lovers or anything. She had no real cause to complain.

Closing his eyes, Fargo willed himself to relax. He could spare a few minutes to rest. Then he would dress and head for the saloon.

"Did you hear something?" Penelope unexpectedly asked.

Fargo had been so deep in thought, he hadn't been paying much attention to the sounds from out in the hall. "Just my blood dripping on the floor."

"What a crybaby." Penelope propped herself up onto her elbows and tilted her head. "But I'm willing to swear blind that I heard someone cry out as if they were in pain."

"Have you made love to anyone else today?" Fargo was feeling as sluggish as a hibernating bear. All he wanted was to snooze a while.

Penelope sat up. "There it was again!"

This time Fargo heard it. A loud *thump* and a gruff outcry. The sounds of a scuffle, coming from the direction of the earl's room. "Damn!" He was up and off the bed in the blink of an eye. Swiftly, he shrugged into his pants, snatched up the Colt, and rushed out the door.

Penelope had pointed out the room earlier. Fargo reached it within seconds and heard the crash of splintering furniture. The door was bolted from within. Stepping back, he threw his shoulder against the panel but it held. He tried again, putting all his weight into it. A rending *crash* resounded, and he burst in.

Two men had paid the earl a nocturnal visit. The top rungs of a ladder propped against an open window explained how they got in. Sherwood was in his nightshirt, on his back on the floor. One attacker had straddled his chest and pinned his shoulders, while the other was hunkered next to his legs, clutching a dagger.

Even as Fargo exploded inward, the man with the dagger sliced the blade into the earl's right leg. Sherwood screeched in pain. The man glanced up at Fargo and shouted, "Stop him, Ernie!" Then he raised the dagger, which was dripping blood, to stab again.

Fargo went to level his revolver but his right foot snagged on the crumpled carpet and he stumbled. Before he could steady himself, the slab of brawn on Sherwood's chest sprang. Sinewy arms clamped around his legs and his feet were yanked out from under him. The next instant he was on his own back, and the man called Ernie was trying to straddle his chest to pin him.

Fargo had other ideas. He drove his knee into Ernie's ribs, knocking him against the wall, clubbed him across the ear and swiveled. The man with the dagger had gained his feet, pulling the earl up with him, and now held the double-edged tip against Sherwood's jugular.

49

"Drop the six-gun or the foreigner dies!"

It was no bluff. The man's eyes told Fargo he had slain before and had no qualms about doing so again.

Sherwood was struggling to break free. "Don't listen to this ruffian! Shoot him! Do you hear? If I die, so be it." Blood was streaming from the two knife wounds, one in each leg.

The man shook the earl like a wolf shaking a marmot. "Keep your mouth shut, you damned dandy! This is between him and me!" The man looked at Fargo again. "What's it going to be?"

Fargo might be able to get off a shot before the dagger was thrust home but he refused to gamble with the Englishman's life. He slowly lowered the Colt. "Let him live and I won't try to stop you."

The man edged toward the doorway, keeping Sherwood between them. "What's it look like out there, Ernie?"

The other was up off the floor, scarlet drops seeping from a nasty gash in his ear. He checked the corridor. "There are three or four heads poking out. Nothing to worry about."

"So far. But it won't be long before they come investigate." The man with the dagger sidled past Fargo, Desmond between them. "We've done our part. Let's get the hell out of here." He backed out of the doorway.

Fargo made no attempt to stop them. "I hope we meet again, you coyote."

"Anytime you're tired of living, look me up." The man lowered the dagger. "You want his highness back, I reckon? Here you go. He's all yours." Chortling, he placed his right boot against the small of the earl's back, and shoved.

Sherwood tried to stay upright but his weakened legs buckled. Raw agony made him cry out.

Fargo caught him before he could hit the floor. "Easy does it."

Boots pounded on the stairs, fading rapidly. Quizzical shouts filled the hallway as Penelope Ashton arrived, breathless and breathtaking. She had thrown on a chemise and her cotton drawers. Over them she wore a sheer nightgown she had neglected to tie.

"Des! What have those animals done to you?"

Fargo carried Sherwood to the settee and carefully set him down. People from other rooms were cautiously peeking in. "Someone fetch a sawbones!" he commanded. "This man has been stabbed."

Sherwood was paler than a sheet. Beads of sweat sprinkled his forehead and he had to swallow a few times before he could speak. "I say, old chap, thank you for another timely intervention." He tried to sit up.

"What in hell do you think you're doing?" Fargo pushed him down again. The earl's night shirt was soaked with blood. Although the wound in his right leg had tapered to a trickle, blood still flowed from the hole in the left. Fargo unfastened the earl's buckle.

"What in bloody hell do you think *you're* doing?" Sherwood demanded.

"We don't want you bleeding to death before the doc gets here." Fargo looped the belt around the earl's left thigh a couple of inches above the wound, then twisted the strap until it was good and tight. The flow immediately stopped.

Penelope clasped Sherwood's hand and kissed his temple. "My sweet, gentle Desmond. Thank God those brutes didn't kill you."

"All they wanted was to keep him from running." And in that, Fargo mused, they had succeeded. Spike Yokum was as persistent as he was heartless.

"My word!" Sherwood grasped Fargo's sleeve. "The other top runners! Promise me you will get word to them tomorrow! They must be warned. There's no predicting who will be next."

"I'll do what I can." Not that Fargo believed it

51

would do much good. The Apache, the Crow woman and Samuels weren't likely to drop out, and as long as they and anyone else Yokum deemed a threat were still in the race, they were at risk.

Sherwood mustered a wan smile for Penelope's benefit. "My mum used to say that cheaters never prosper. I would hate to think she was wrong."

"Mark my words, Des. The blighter responsible will pay." Penelope's eyes were misting over. Her quirks in bed aside, she sincerely cared for her friend.

"It's my own fault for leaving the window open to get some fresh air." Sherwood patted her hand. "Six months from now I'll be right as rain."

Fargo frowned. By then the footrace would be long over, and Spike Yokum would be ten thousand dollars richer. The hypocrite. Yokum had Harley killed because the gunman caused trouble, yet here Yokum was, stirring up even more. Maybe Yokum justified it because it was *his* doing.

One thing was for sure.

This wasn't over.

The worst might be yet to come.

5

"That must have been some fight you were in, hand-some," Marta said, bending down to caress Fargo's brow. "I'm just happy you weren't hurt, like that nice British gent. Stabbed in both legs, you say?"

"I could use more whiskey." Fargo hefted his empty glass. It was close to midnight, and they were in her small, but comfortably furnished, apartment. He didn't like deceiving her. None of his bruises and cuts were the result of the scrape with the earl's attackers. But he doubted she would take it very well were he to reveal he had been delayed because of his romp with Penelope Ashton.

"Sure thing." Marta scooted to a cabinet. "I was getting worried there for a while. Afraid maybe you had changed your mind about spending the night with me."

"That wouldn't happen in a million years," Fargo heard himself say.

"Are you sure you're up to it, though?" Marta deposited the glass back in his hand and herself in his lap. "That cheek of yours is pretty swollen. Here. Maybe this will help." She kissed it, and grinned. "When I was little, my ma would kiss my hurts to make them better. Hurties, she liked to call them."

Fargo's thoughts raced to his own childhood. Painful memories washed over him, until finally he banished them from his mind with a toss of his head.

Marta misconstrued. "Hey, if you don't want to take a tumble under the sheets, I understand. You must be sore all over."

"It's not that—" Fargo caught himself. He wasn't *that* bruised. And it *had* been several hours.

"What? You're thinking of sweet Mr. Sherwood? How he'll be laid up for a couple of weeks?"

Fargo was glad she was so great at jumping to conclusions. He played along. "The doctor said it could be a year before he's able to run again."

Marta looped an arm around his neck. She still had on her tight green dress, and perfume wreathed her like the natural fragrance of a rose wreathed its petals. "Do you really think Spike Yokum had something to do with it? I know he's snake mean and all, but he's always been one to keep a low profile."

"Ten thousand dollars is a lot of money."

"And most people would do anything to get their hands on that much. Is that what you're saying?"

Despite himself, Fargo smiled and kissed her. "You read minds better than anyone I've ever met."

Marta beamed and snuggled closer, her ample breasts cushioned against his shirt. "I've always had a knack. Ever since I was a little girl. My pa used to claim I was an expert at putting words in other people's mouths."

Fargo bit his lower lip to keep from agreeing and regretted it when it flared with pain. He had forgotten what Penelope did.

"Oh, you poor thing, you," Marta said. She kissed his bottom lip, then his upper, then his left cheek, his right. Tiny kisses, they were. Nibbles that sent tingles of pleasure rippling clear to his toes. "Feeling any better yet?" she playfully asked.

Fargo was feeling a lot better. He was warm all over, and a familiar twitching below his belt proved he still had some fire in the furnace. Idly caressing her silken hair, he leaned his head back, closed his eyes, and let her have her way with him.

Marta removed his hat and ran her fingers through his hair, then lavished a hundred and one moist kisses on his face and neck. Each was as soft as a feather, as light as air. She was talented, this lady. Her hot lips roamed to his earlobe and she enveloped it in the satiny swirl of her tongue. Her touch was magically soft, as different from Penelope Ashton as water was from rock.

The tension draining from his body, Fargo relished every second. He felt her tug at his buckskin shirt and helped her slowly ease it up over his head.

"Look at all these muscles!" Marta cooed, sculpting his washboard abdomen with her palms. Her hands were as soft as her lips. "You're gorgeous!"

Fargo lost himself in sweet sensation. He was adrift on a tranquil sea, oblivious to everything except her wonderfully stimulating mouth and fingers. She nibbled and licked from his neck to his right shoulder, then down across his chest to his nipple. He heard her giggle, then her mouth was doing to him what his had been doing to Penelope not all that long ago. Any lingering doubts he had about his manhood being up for it evaporated as his pants bulged.

Marta was marvelous. She took supreme delight in giving him pleasure. Her skill with her mouth was incredible. She could do things not one woman in fifty could do; in the way she kneaded his skin, the way she rolled it, the way she would suck it up into her mouth and then gently release him.

Fargo lost all track of time. A low groan filled the room and he realized it was his. His boots were slid off. Fingers plucked at his gun belt, at his pants. He rose high enough in the chair for her to take them off. Stark naked, he sat back down.

Marta's lips fastened on his thigh. Gossamer wings

flitted down one leg and up the other. Warm, wet wings, that gave birth to shiver after shiver. Was it an hour later, or was it two, when Marta's mouth rose to his and fastened in a kiss that plumbed his core?

Fargo opened his eyes to find she had shed her garments. Her breasts brushed his chest, her palms rubbed his back. She was as tender and soft as Penelope had been fierce and hard.

Fargo embraced her and rose. Sliding his left arm under her bottom, he carried her to the bed. Her mounds were fuller, her hips wider, than Penelope's. Her legs were longer yet every bit as nicely contoured. Only around the eyes had her life as a dove taken its inevitable toll in the form of small crow's feet. Minor flaws or testaments to her character, depending on whether her cup was regarded as half empty or half full.

Fargo had never been one to look down his nose at others. He never judged anyone on other than their own merits. Not everyone felt that way. 'Good people' in every town he had ever been in weren't as open-minded. To them, a woman like Marta was a sinner doomed to perdition, a worthless tramp, a blight on the community.

To Fargo, Marta and her ilk were no worse than anyone else. Ordinary folk, caught up in circumstances over which they had no control and making what they could of their lives. Marta had remarked that given her druthers she would do something different. But jobs for women, particularly decent jobs, were few and far between. Like so many wives suddenly made widows, she had fallen into the only niche open to her. She had to eat, she needed a roof over her head. Casting blame, Fargo reckoned, wasn't called for.

Marta was nibbling at his throat. Her hands were farther down, her fingers where they would excite him the most. She hadn't spoken in a while, but now, raising her head, she commented, "Has anyone ever told you that you have a fine body? Some men are all flab. You're all muscle."

Fargo placed his hand over her left breast. "You have a fine body, yourself. How about if I show you the parts I like best?"

Marta grinned. "I'd like that. Just don't be rough. I never have liked it when a man gets carried away." She touched a small scar. "This is what I got the last time it happened."

Sliding his mouth to her other nipple, Fargo did his best to arouse her as she had aroused him. He spent long minutes kissing and tweaking. He slipped a hand between her thighs and stroked them, but he held off touching her innermost core. He wanted her desire to build, for her to crave him to the point where she couldn't get enough.

More moans wafted to the ceiling. Marta's, this time. Her legs rubbed his, her hands roved at their leisure. Her eyes half-closed, she squirmed nonstop. She was a ripe peach waiting to be eaten.

With that in mind, Fargo knelt and applied his mouth to her. Marta arched up off the bed and gave voice to a husky cry of breathless need. Sinking down, she clasped her arms to her bosom and quivered in ecstasy as he transported her to the heights, and beyond.

"Oh! Oh! Yessss!"

With that, Marta spurted. Her whole body bucked upward, her thighs a vise against his ears.

Fargo didn't stop until his tongue was sore and she was as limp as a wet rag. Then, rubbing his pole along her honey box, he positioned himself on his knees. Rather than take her hard and fast, as he had Penelope, he inserted himself inch by ever-so-slow inch.

A sigh that was more than a sigh escaped Marta's puckered red lips. Awash in a look of total contentment, she held herself completely still in breathless anticipation.

So did Fargo, until the ache in his loins was unbearable and his member was fit to explode. He rocked in the ages-old rhythm of human coupling, the rhythm of flesh on flesh, of two forms joined as one.

Fargo's release took forever. He had seldom lasted so long. Whether it was due to her tender lovemaking or his recent frolic with Penelope or both was unclear. Presently, his manhood could no longer be denied, so when a paroxysm of rapture seized her, he let the floodgates down.

Later, much later, after they had coasted to a breathless stop, Marta whispered, "Thank you. You're a magnificent lover."

"I just do what comes naturally," Fargo made light of his ability. Stretching out beside her, he draped an arm across her shoulders and within seconds had dozed off. His sleep was dreamless and undisturbed. When he awoke at sunrise, as he invariably did, he felt immensely refreshed, and famished enough to eat a buffalo.

Marta snored softly, strands of hair across her angelic face.

As carefully as if he were lying on eggshells, Fargo rolled off of the bed so as not to awaken her. Soon he was dressed, his hat on his head. He admired her for a moment, then quietly worked the bolt and slipped out.

Nugget still dozed. A few roosters were crowing, and down the street a shopkeeper was sweeping the boardwalk in front of his store.

Only fourteen runners were at the starting point when Fargo trotted up on the Ovaro, among them Amarillo, Swift Fox and Samuels. They weren't stretching and limbering up as runners usually did. They were clustered in small groups, talking.

"Is it true what we heard?" Luther Samuels demanded the moment Fargo alighted. "The Brit is out of the race?"

"Unless he can run on his hands." Fargo was interested in learning how they found out about the attack.

"The story is all over town," Samuels replied. "Some are sayin' the race should be postponed a few days. Others are callin' for it to be canceled."

"Is it also true you were there?" Swift Fox asked.

Fargo recounted the two attacks, ending with, "The marshal promised to get to the bottom of it. But if the person I suspect is behind the attacks, he's covered his tracks really well."

"And who would that be?" Around a nearby boulder came Spike Yokum, his suit immaculate. With him were Silvermane and Mitch. Plus one other. A man an inch or two over six feet, with close-cropped black hair, an athletic build and an arrogant swagger. He wore a beige running outfit. "I want the culprit caught as much as the next man."

"Sure you do," Fargo said.

Yokum took the barb in stride. "Permit me to introduce Richard Thorne. Perhaps you have heard of him? He's one of the premier runners in the country. Won more events than any man living. Or any woman." He gave Swift Fox a pointed look.

Thorne didn't bother to shake. "It's a pity about Sherwood. He's the one person who might have given me a challenge."

Samuels pulled his floppy hat lower. "You haven't won yet, sucker. Say that again after you've swallowed my dust."

"The day I can't beat a darkie is the day I take up needlepoint," Thorne snapped.

Incensed, Samuels took a step, but he stopped when Silvermane moved between them. The small gunman's hands were a whisker from the pearl grips on his Smith and Wessons.

"Now, now, Mr. Samuels," Spike Yokum said, wagging a thick finger. "There will be none of that. Mr.

Thorne has entered the race at my request, and it wouldn't sit well with me were he to come to harm."

"You don't scare me none!" Samuels blustered, but he didn't make an issue of it.

Richard Thorne nodded at the trail. Wooden stakes four feet high had been added since yesterday to mark the official course. "Time to see whether this race is worthy of my talents. I'll meet you at your saloon later, Yokum."

"I don't care if this is just practice, he ain't beatin' me," Samuels growled, and jogged after him.

The other runners took that as their cue. Not Swift Fox, though. She glanced at Fargo and beckoned him to one side. "Among my people it is said He-Who-Tracks always speaks with a straight tongue. That unlike others of your kind, you never lie."

"That's not entirely true," Fargo admitted.

Swift Fox squinted up at him. "You are honest at heart, whether you admit it or not. So tell me, He-Who-Tracks. Is Sherwood the last? Or will others be harmed before tomorrow morning?"

"The one you should ask is Spike Yokum." Fargo saw Yokum staring at them. "Does he strike you as the kind who likes to lose?"

The maiden shook her head. "He strikes me as a wolverine. Gluttons, your people call them, because they never get enough. Yokum is like that. He wants it all, and he will destroy anyone who gets in his way." She moved toward the first marker. "Perhaps we will talk again."

"I'd like that," Fargo said as a shadow moved across him.

"Did I hear my name mentioned?" Yokum's smile was as fake as a counterfeit bill. Silvermane was at his right elbow, Mitch on the left. "I don't much like having people talk about me behind my back. Mind telling me what that was about?"

"I was telling her what an upstanding citizen you

are." Fargo clapped him on the arm. "Hell, if it weren't for you, Nugget wouldn't have half the killings and muggings it does."

"Pettiness ill becomes you." Yokum's features had clouded. "Am I to assume from your tone that you have decided to decline my offer?"

"Does sitting on a cactus hurt?"

"I can't say as I'm surprised. But why have you turned me down? Are you afraid I can't afford your services?"

"If you can afford this runt," Fargo nodded at Silvermane, "you can afford to hire just about anyone."

"So it's not the money. What then?"

"One of three rules I have."

"Rules?" Yokum was clearly perplexed. "A man like you? Your fondness for booze and cards is as well known as your fondness for anything in skirts. What sort of rules could you have?"

For each one Fargo mentioned, he held up a finger. "One, never play against a stacked deck. Two, never stand in front of stampeding buffalo. And three, never work for a son of a bitch."

Spike Yokum's jaw muscles bulged and his huge hands formed into mallets. For a moment Fargo thought he would take a swing at him but all Yokum did was slide a cigar from a jacket pocket, jam it into his mouth, and angrily tromp toward the horses. Mitch fell into step behind him like a well-trained guard dog but Silvermane lingered.

"I've never met anyone who makes as many bone-headed mistakes as you do. You must have a death wish. Insulting Mr. Yokum is the second-worst thing you could have done. The worst was calling me a runt."

"Your mother has me beat. She gave birth to you."

The small gunman's mouth fell open like a sprung trapdoor. He was rooted in astonishment, but not for long. "You *dare* talk to *me* like that?"

"Would you rather I use sign language?"

Silvermane backed up several steps, hatred animating his features. "Mister, you've just dug yourself a grave. Your rep means nothing to me. I've killed twenty-seven men in my time."

"Is that all?" Fargo was deliberately provoking him. Rage made a gunman reckless, and he needed an edge, any edge, to come out on top against a quick-draw artist as talented as this one.

It worked. Silvermane was literally quaking with fury. "Whenever you're ready!" he snarled.

Fargo had another barb on the tip of his tongue but fate intervened with a shout from the gunfighter's employer.

"Silvermane! Enough! Have you forgotten that you work for me? I will choose the time and place, if you please."

Tension crackled like heat lightning. Fargo didn't know if the small gunman would listen or go for his hardware anyway. Maybe one last insult would do the trick. "Better tuck your tail between your legs and slink over to your master."

A strange thing happened. Instead of clawing at his revolvers, Silvermane slowly unfurled, a lopsided grin creasing his face. "Clever, hombre. Real clever. You got me so mad I wasn't thinking straight. I acted like a damned greenhorn."

"So if I say your mother was a drunken whore it won't upset you?"

"Why should it?" Silvermane turned. "She *was one.* Nice try, though." He headed for the horses. "We'll meet again. Only next time I'll decide how this ends."

Fargo watched until they were out of sight, then forked leather and lifted the reins to return to town. He happened to gaze westward and for the briefest instant spied a bright flash of light. It was there, then it was gone. As if the sun had been reflected off of a mirror. Or metal.

Disturbed, Fargo reined west rather than east. The

spot was close to the race route. He should make sure it was nothing. For about a mile he paralleled the trail, holding to a brisk walk. Only once did he see the runners, far ahead.

The flash of light had been on a rise. It was there Fargo found hoofprints and the boot tracks of a lone rider who had dismounted and crouched to watch the runners go by. Then the rider mounted his horse and climbed sloping ground toward a broad shelf that overlooked a long stretch of the course.

Odds were it was someone planning to bet on the outcome, there to evaluate how the runners performed. But it could just as well be someone up to no good. Fargo brought the Ovaro to a trot. Rising in the stirrups occasionally to scour the landscape, he lucked out and spotted the other rider before the rider noticed him.

The man was atop the shelf. He had dismounted and was peering over the rim, probably at the runners, a hand over his eyes to shield them from the sun. He was holding a rifle.

Circling to the south, Fargo came up on the rifleman from behind. When he was a hundred yards out he drew rein, slid off, and shucked his Henry from its saddle scabbard. Working the lever, he fed a cartridge into the chamber and cat-footed to a steep incline covered with loose earth and rocks. Footholds were treacherous at best but it was the only way up.

Fargo climbed rapidly, frowning every time stones and dirt rattled from under his boots. The slope became so steep three-fourths of the way up that he had to tuck the Henry under his arm and use his hands for added balance. Only five feet separated him from the rim when the *crack* of a shot told him he was too late.

His boots churning, Fargo gained the top. Boulders were everywhere, blocking his view. He skirted several and spied the man's horse, a dun.

The rifleman was in the act of climbing on. Whipping the weapon to his shoulder, the man snapped off a hasty shot that missed.

Fargo's answering shot didn't. He saw the rider pitch from the dun and fall out of sight behind a boulder. The horse shied and trotted a short distance eastward. Fargo hurried toward it, never taking his eyes off the saddle. If the gunman were still alive, he would make another bid to escape.

Rounding a last boulder, Fargo saw the dun clearly. The rifleman was nowhere around. He glanced at the spot where the body should be lying but it wasn't there.

"Looking for me?"

A gun hammer clicked to his rear, and Fargo froze.

"Drop the Henry and turn around. I want you to see it coming when I blow out your wick."

Fargo found himself staring down the large-bore barrel of a .55 caliber Jennings Magazine Rifle. Rare on the frontier, they used percussion caps and had a ring trigger few frontiersmen liked. Nevertheless, they were as lethal as his Henry or any other gun.

"Figures it would be you," the man spat. "I was warned you were meddling where you shouldn't."

To Fargo's knowledge they had never met before. "Should I know you? Do you work for Spike Yokum?"

"Did I say you could talk?" The gunman took a step. Scarlet splotches stained his shirt high on the right shoulder, and he had lost his hat when he fell. "All you should care about is that I'm about to blow your brains out."

Fargo's only hope was to unlimber his Colt. But the rifleman would fire before he cleared leather, and, at that range, couldn't miss.

"Worried now, aren't you? I can see it in your eyes."

Stall! Fargo mentally railed at himself. *Stall him or*

you're dead. "You shot one of the runners, didn't you?"

"I hope so. It's what I've been paid to do. But some sweat got into my eyes." The man mopped at his forehead but the rifle never wavered. "What the hell am I doing, jabbering like this? It must be the shock of being hit."

"A condemned man always gets a last request. I'd like to know who you work for."

"This ain't a prison, and I ain't no warden."

Fargo glanced down. If he could kick up some dust, or send a rock flying, anything to distract him.

The gunman pressed his cheek to the stock and sighted down the barrel. "There's a bonus for killing you. Five hundred dollars. Ten days from now I'll be in San Francisco spending it on fine fillies and finer Scotch, and I'll drink a toast in your honor."

"You're all heart."

"Ain't I though?" The assassin's finger tightened.

6

Skye Fargo's reflexes were second to none but even he couldn't dodge a bullet. Yet that's exactly what he tried to do. It was either that, or stand there and be gunned down, and he had never counted meekness as one of his qualities. *Eye for an eye* was his philosophy. Surviving at all costs was his nature. So when he saw the gunman's finger begin to curl around the ring trigger, he threw himself to the right and grabbed for his Colt.

The Jennings Magazine Rifle boomed. A hornet buzzed Fargo's ear. He streaked his revolver out, but a fraction of a second before he fired, the gunman skipped to one side. His slug went wide. Landing hard on his shoulder, he elevated the Colt to fire again but another shot wasn't necessary.

The killer was stock-still, face rigid, the Jennings Magazine Rifle drooping in hands gone weak. Two arrows were the cause, feathered shafts imbedded halfway in his rib cage. He looked at Fargo, croaked, "What the hell?" and died without ever learning who slew him.

The next moment one of the Apaches Fargo had seen in town stepped into the open. It was the one with the bow, another shaft nocked to the string. Paying Fargo no mind, the Mimbre walked over to the gunman and nudged the prone figure with a toe, ensuring it was lifeless.

Fargo had been mistaken when he told Spike Yokum there were three rules he lived by. There was a fourth. Never let down his guard around Apaches. Especially the wilder ones, like the Mimbres. As he rose, he leveled the Colt, just in case. "Do you speak the white man's tongue?"

"He does not. I do."

When Fargo glanced over his shoulder, he saw that the other Apache, the warrior with the Sharps, had the carbine trained on his back. "I'm not your enemy," he stated.

The Apache gestured at the dead gunman. "We know." He lowered the Sharps and moved past Fargo to his friend's side. "This one shot at Amarillo."

"How bad was he hit?" Fargo turned toward the trail. Down below, heads were poking over boulders and from behind bushes.

"The white-eye missed."

The Mimbre with the bow handed it to the other, drew his bone-handled hunting knife, and sank to his knees.

"Don't!" Fargo could guess what the warrior was up to. Most Apache bands believed that if they mutilated an enemy, the enemy's spirit suffered accordingly in the afterlife. Cut out the eyes, and the enemy was blind. Cut off the fingers, and the enemy had useless stubs.

Both Mimbres looked up.

"Think of the white-eyes in town," Fargo said. "Even if this one deserves it, they'll hold it against you. Maybe make trouble for Amarillo. Do you want that?"

A short palaver resulted. The one holding the knife stood up and reluctantly sheathed his blade.

"You give wise advice," his companion said. "We need prize."

Fargo picked up the Henry. "Since when do Apaches care about the white man's money? Your

67

people have shunned contact with whites for years."
Like the Sioux and the Blackfeet, the Comanches and
the Bloods, the Apaches saw the whites as invaders
who should be driven out.

The Mimbre patted his Sharps. "Money buy many
new guns. Many bullets. Makes our band strong.
Stronger than other tribes. Stronger than Mexicans.
Stronger than Blue Coats. Strongest of all." Without
another word the pair turned and jogged in among
the boulders.

Fargo burst out laughing, struck by the irony of
using white money to buy white guns to kill whites.
Only Apaches would be so delightfully devious.

A shout from below intruded on his amusement.
"Fargo? Is that you up there? What the devil is
going on?"

Luther Samuels, Swift Fox, and five other runners
had emerged from concealment. Of Amarillo, interest-
ingly enough, there was no sign.

Cupping a hand to his mouth, Fargo answered, "It
was a bushwhacker! He's dead! It's safe to go on!"

Nodding, Samuels and the rest resumed their practice run. But not Swift Fox. She came up the shelf in
those long, graceful strides of hers that ate up the
distance as fast as a bounding deer. Despite the fact
she had been running for over half an hour under a
broiling hot sun, she wasn't sweating or breathing all
that heavily. "Shouldn't you be with the rest?"

"I will catch up." Swift Fox gazed past him. "Is this
more of Spike Yokum's handiwork?"

"Maybe we can find out." Fargo went to the body
and squatted.

The maiden came closer. "Surely he would not be
careless enough to have something on him that would
prove who hired him?"

"You never know." Fargo delved his fingers into
the deceased's pockets. A folding knife, a handful of
coins, and tobacco were all he found until he inspected

an inner pocket of the man's cowhide vest. "What have we here?" It was a wad of bills. Unfolding them, he whistled softly. "Seven hundred dollars."

"Only someone like Yokum could afford to pay that much," Swift Fox remarked.

"There's a lot of silver money floating around Nugget," Fargo reminded her, stuffing money into his own pocket.

"You defend an animal with no scruples? I expected better of one who has always treated my people with respect."

Fargo had encountered more than a few Crows in his travels, and for the most part the meetings had been peaceful. "All I'm suggesting is that it never pays to jump to conclusions." He stood.

"Will you ride guard over us the rest of the way?"

"No need. Thanks to Amarillo, you already have a pair of guardian angels watching over you."

"I suspected as much, unless you have a bow hidden under your shirt." Swift Fox pointed at the arrows, then faced him. "My people are camped northeast of town. We would be honored if you would pay us a visit this evening. Say about sunset?" She didn't wait for an answer.

Cradling the Henry, Fargo admired how her beaded dress highlighted the sweep of her thighs and her backside. He wouldn't mind spending a night in her company. For now, though, he retrieved the dun, hoisted the dead man onto his shoulder, and draped it over the saddle. Sliding the Jennings Magazine Rifle into its scabbard, he grabbed the reins and searched for an easier way down.

The Ovaro was right where it should be. Mounting, Fargo hightailed it for town.

As usual the streets bustled with activity, most of which ground to a halt. The body created quite a stir. Men stared, women put their hands to their mouths, mothers made their children avert their eyes.

The marshal's office was near the edge of town but Fargo rode on by. He had another destination in mind; a hitch rail in front of the Motherlode Saloon. One of Yokum's gunhands lost no time in rushing inside to report his arrival to the big man himself.

Fargo pushed through the doors and stepped to the left so his back was to the wall. The place had gone totally quiet. All eyes were on him as he moved toward the bar. Many of those lining it decided it was wiser to be elsewhere.

Near the far end stood Spike Yokum, talking to Silvermane. Nearby were Mitch and the gunman who had dashed in to warn them.

"Whiskey," Fargo said to the bartender.

Yokum's curiosity was showing. "Talk about surprises. To what do I owe this dubious honor?"

"I brought a friend of yours to see you." Fargo nodded at the entrance. "He couldn't make it in on his own."

"A friend?" Yokum's eyebrows pinched together. He motioned to Mitch and the other hard case. "Go see what he's babbling about."

The bartender set a full glass down. Fargo forked out the roll of bills he had taken from the assassin and made a show of unfolding them. Out of the corner of his eye he watched Yokum's reaction. For if it was Yokum who hired him, then Yokum was bound to realize where the money came from.

The big man never batted an eye.

Disappointed, Fargo paid and returned the money to his pocket. Either Yokum had nothing to do with it or he was the best actor on the planet.

"Being a scout must pay better than I thought. Or have you taken up mugging as a hobby?"

"You're in a good mood." Fargo polished off the red-eye in several quick gulps to wash the dust from his throat.

"Why shouldn't I be? By tomorrow night our illustrious mayor will be eating crow. I can't wait to see the look on his chubby face when Thorne wins."

"And there's always the ten thousand," Fargo mentioned.

Yokum snorted. "A paltry sum, of no interest to me. I've promised Thorne he can keep the purse if he wins. The added incentive should do wonders to enhance his performance."

"You don't want the prize money for yourself?"

"Be serious," Yokum scoffed. "Between this saloon and my other enterprises, including a quarter-interest in the most profitable mine in the territory, I make more than that in any given month. My only interest in winning is to put Quinby in his place."

Fargo wrestled with the revelation. "The earl was almost crippled for *that*?"

Yokum drew up to his full height. "First of all, I've never admitted having any part in the Englishman's unfortunate maiming. Second, if I were, I'd have no regrets. I'll do anything to get the better of Quinby. Anything!

"Bad blood between the two of you, is that it?"

"Trailsman, you don't know the half of it. I was here first. My saloon was the first in town. My money helped over a dozen business get off the ground. I've done more on Nugget's behalf than Quinby ever will. If anyone deserves to be mayor, it's me. Not that miserable snake in the grass." As Yokum talked he became more and more agitated, until now he pounded the bar so loud, customers for yards around turned. "The only thing Quinby can do better than me is talk rings around trees. He's a natural-born politician. You should have seen him before the election! Praising himself to high heaven and kissing babies like there was no tomorrow."

Fargo's estimation of his honor, the mayor, dropped several degrees. Little did he know it was about to drop a lot further.

"And you! Looking down your nose at me for bringing Richard Thorne in to run the race on my behalf. What about Quinby? Have you taken him to task for sending for the Englishman?"

"Wait a minute. Are you saying the earl was running for Quinby?"

"You didn't know?" Yokum uttered a few choice swear words. "I was content to let the best person win. But when I heard our stuffed shirt of a mayor had brought in Desmond Sherwood, I decided to fight fire with fire and contacted Thorne."

Fargo needed another drink. Nothing was as it had seemed. The whole situation had to be viewed in a new light that didn't bode well for the other fleet runners.

Mitch and the gunman returned.

"Well?" Yokum prodded when they stood there like a pair of simpletons.

"It's some dead hombre, boss," Mitch replied. "We never set eyes on him before. He's not on your payroll, I can tell you that much."

There it was, Fargo reflected. Added proof things were a lot worse than he thought.

Spike Yokum was puzzled. "Care to explain what this was all about? Who's out there? And why did you think he was one of mine?"

"My mistake." Fargo turned to leave but Yokum wasn't letting him off the hook that easy. A mallet-sized hand gripped his arm and spun him partway around.

"Hold it. You're the one who marched in here all high and mighty. All I'm asking for is an explanation."

Silvermane was sidling to the left for a clear shot while Mitch and the other gunhand moved to the right.

Fargo ignored them for the moment. They wouldn't slap leather without a direct command from Yokum.

"Fair enough. The dead man tried to shoot the Apache runner, Amarillo."

"And you naturally assumed he was working for me?" Yokum wasn't flattered. "Go to hell. And while you're at it, go ask Quinby if he was behind it. He's got as much at stake as I do."

"I think I will." Walking backward to keep his eyes on them, Fargo reached the street.

A crowd had gathered around the hitch rail. Pushing through it was Marshal Tom Darnell. He raised the assassin's head, he studied the face a moment, then commented, "Has anyone ever told you, Mr. Fargo, that you draw trouble like garbage draws flies?" He unwound the dun's reins from the rail. "I saw you ride past my office a while ago. Follow me, if you would. You have a heap of explaining to do."

"So everyone keeps saying," Fargo replied.

Frontier towns were notorious for not placing too high a premium on law and order. They hired anyone willing to pin on tin and paid the walking targets peanuts. Then they added insult to insult by providing offices no bigger than an outhouse. Marshal Darnell had room for a small desk, an old chair, and a cot on which he deposited the recently departed.

"No jail cell?" Fargo remarked. It wasn't uncommon. Many towns were too stingy with their tax dollars to foot the expense.

"The council says they'll get around to having one built one of these days." The lawman sank into the chair. "In the meantime, there's a woodshed out back that makes do." He jabbed a thumb at the body. "Start talking."

Ten minutes later the lawman pushed his hat back and scowled. "It sounds to me like Spike Yokum is up to his usual tricks. Someone would be doing Nugget a great favor if they were to put him out of our misery." He winked slyly.

Pretending to be interested in something out the

window, Fargo stepped closer to the desk. Then, whirling, he lunged and seized the lawman by the front of the shirt. "I'm on to you now. Mayor Quinby would like nothing better than for me to go gunning for Yokum. And your job is to trick me into doing it."

Momentarily speechless, Darnell swiftly recovered his composure and tried to pry Fargo's fingers off. "What the hell do you think you're doing? I could throw you in the woodshed for this!"

"I'd like to see you try." Fargo pushed Darnell toward the wall.

Chair and lawman tumbled. The marshal ended up with his legs entangled, squawking, "You're under arrest!" He clutched at his sidearm.

Fargo was faster. He kicked Darnell's wrist, sending the revolver skidding across the floor. Darnell yelped, then came up swinging. Fargo absorbed a blow to the stomach that wouldn't bend a blade of grass. His own punch folded the marshal over, and Darnell lay wheezing in mixed anger and fear. Slowly drawing the Colt, Fargo touched the muzzle to Darnell's temple.

"Don't! Please!"

"Do you know the one thing worse than an outlaw? A lawman who doesn't abide by the law."

"I don't have any idea what you're talking about," Darnell snarled.

"Like hell you don't. You've been leading me on since we met. Painting Yokum as the worst polecat this side of the Divide, and all the time Mayor Quinby has been pulling your strings." Fargo rose and took a step back. "Give the mayor a message for me. Tell him he'll have to find someone else to do his killing."

Fargo had made another enemy. Darnell's fury-filled gaze followed him to the door.

"You want some advice, mister? Get on that pinto of yours and make yourself scarce. You've stuck your nose in things that don't concern you." The lawman gripped the desk to pull himself up. "The mayor might strike you as a fool but he's not. He can be as dangerous as Yokum when his dander is up, and he'll be after your hide for this."

Fargo didn't doubt it. But one more out to get him hardly mattered. Quinby could get in line behind Yokum and Silvermane. He slammed the door, went half a block, and stopped in the shade of an overhang to ponder.

The marshal had been right about one thing. The race was none of his concern. He had no vested interest in risking his neck. So why stay? It wasn't as if any of the runners meant anything to him. He'd liked the earl, but Sherwood had been in the mayor's hip pocket the whole time. Luther Samuels was a clod with a temper. Amarillo was only in the race to get guns for his people. Richard Thorne was a jackass.

That left Swift Fox. Fargo had to admit he was attracted to her, but he also had to be careful it didn't cloud his judgement. She seemed innocent enough, but she might have a deep, dark secret of her own.

Maybe he really should climb on the Ovaro and light a shuck. No one would be sorry to see him go. Quite the contrary. Yokum and Quinby would be delighted. Which in itself was more than enough reason to stay. The mayor had tried to trick him into gunning Yokum, and Yokum had tried to buy him off with the offer of a high-paying job. They were users, the kind who ran roughshod over people and never gave it a second thought. Both deserved to be given a taste of their own bitter medicine, and he was just the one to do it.

Since there was plenty of time to kill until evening, Fargo made his way to the saloon where Marta worked. She hadn't shown up yet. Out of habit he sat in on a poker game but it was hard to concentrate on the cards when every time the batwing doors opened it might be a gunman sent by Yokum or Quinby.

Along about noon Marta waltzed in. She came right

over and planted a moist kiss on his cheek. "Why didn't you wake me before you left?" she whispered. "I love to start the day making hay."

"I'll make it up to you tonight," Fargo promised. He didn't mention his visit later to the Crow camp. She might not like the idea of Swift Fox's invitation.

Marta giggled. "You won't be disappointed. I haven't enjoyed being with a man so much since I can't remember when."

A loud commotion outside brought all conversation and play to a halt. There was a lot of yelling. Boots thumped heavily. Everyone glanced toward the doors just as an out-of-breath grungy prospector burst in.

"Did you folks hear? One of the runners might be out of the race. He's been bit by a rattlesnake!"

Murmuring broke out. Almost every man in town was wagering on the outcome.

"Who was it, do you know?" a gambler asked.

"Sure do," the prospector said. "It's that Thorne character, the one who just got in. They're taking him to the doc's right this moment. He's in a bad way, from what I understand."

Fargo had to find out for himself. Raking in his money, he asked Marta for directions. Dozens of people were already there, clamoring for news of Thorne's condition. He hung back until he spotted Spike Yokum and Mayor Quinby in a heated argument.

"—dare you accuse me of having a hand in this!" the mayor declared as Fargo pushed forward to overhear. "Blame the Almighty, not me! A rattler is His handiwork, not mine. Thorne's mishap is divine Providence, you might say."

Yokum was livid. "Hell! You wouldn't know divinity if it jumped up and bit you on your fat ass! If I find this was your doing, the town council will need to call a special election to pick your replacement."

"Don't use that tone on me!" Quinby rasped. "I'll put up with a lot of things but not that. Not in public."

"You'll put up with whatever I say you will, you miserable—"

Yokum never finished his statement. The door to the doctor's office opened and out walked a gray-haired gentleman, his shirtsleeves rolled up, wiping his hands on a white cloth. Quiet descended, broken by Yokum demanding, "What's the verdict, doc? Can he take part in the race or not?"

"Is that all you care about?" the physician answered.

"If you had as much riding on the race as I do, you would feel the same," Yokum defended himself.

"I seriously doubt that. But be that as it may." The doctor surveyed those assembled. "Richard Thorne is fortunate to be alive. He was bitten in the left calf. One of the snake's fangs punctured a vein, and the poison has spread throughout his body. He'll recover, given time, but he won't be able to walk for days, much less do any running."

"Did he say how it happened?" Yokum probed.

From out of the crowd stepped Luther Samuels and Swift Fox. "We can answer that," the black man declared. "We were only a little ways behind him when it happened. There wasn't anything anyone could do."

"I'll be the judge of that." Yokum speared a finger at the Crow maiden. "What about it, squaw? You're the only one who doesn't have a vested interest. Let's hear your version."

Swift Fox stiffened. "Do not call me that."

"What? Squaw? I didn't mean to offend you. Whites call your kind squaws all the time."

"That does not make it right."

Samuels was looking from one to the other, and he wasn't happy. "How come you'll only listen to her? Why not hear what I have to say? Is it the color of my skin?"

"What if it is?" was Yokum's blunt response. "It's a free country and I can do as I damn well please."

77

He had not taken his eyes off Swift Fox. "I'm waiting, lady, and I don't have all day."

"There is not much to say. We were near the end of our practice run. Mr. Thorne was in front of us. No one noticed a rattlesnake coiled beside the trail until it bit him. We did what we could, then brought him here. That is all."

Spike Yokum glared. At her, at Samuels, at the doctor, then at the doctor's office. He stormed off but had only taken a few steps when he saw Fargo, and halted. The oddest expression came over him, and he gave voice to an equally odd statement. "It's a long shot. But we can't always go with thoroughbreds, much as we'd like to." The next moment he was barreling through the crowd.

Now what was that all about? Fargo mused. Whatever sparked it, he had the distinct feeling it didn't bode well.

7

Swift Fox had said the Crow camp was northeast of town. She hadn't said how far.

An hour out of Nugget Fargo came to a bluff. His first instinct was to go around to save time even though the tracks he had been following wound toward the rim. He doubted the Crows were up there. It was too open, too exposed. Then again, it was an ideal vantage point. No one could get anywhere near them without being spotted. As he sat there debating what to do, a shadow detached itself from a cluster of boulders.

"I was beginning to think you would not come."

Fargo nodded at the blazing orange orb perched on the horizon. "By sunset, you said. I'm right on time."

Swift Fox was as radiant as ever. "Follow me. My people are expecting you." She climbed with the same grace she always displayed when she ran, her figure as alluring as a pot of honey to a hungry bear.

Mentally clamping a lid on his desire, Fargo tried not to pay undue attention to her mouth-watering contours. He failed.

At the top Fargo drew rein in mild surprise. Four lodges had been erected, typical tepees of buffalo hide. Not far off was a small spring. Tethered close to it, enclosed within a rope corral, were dozens of horses. Over twenty Crows were waiting; warriors, women and children. None of the warriors were armed, an encouraging sign.

The Crow tribe was peaceful enough toward whites, although over the years a few violent incidents had occurred. Most in the early days of the fur trade, when whites and the red man were first becoming acquainted. The general rule of thumb for dealing with them was to be friendly but not to let down one's guard.

Swift Fox and an older man were talking. The gray-haired one smiled and his hands flowed in sign language. Essentially, he said, "Welcome, He-Who-Tracks. Our lodges are your lodges. Our food is your food. Our water is your water."

"I am glad to call you friend," Fargo responded. It struck him as peculiar how they were all staring so intently, as if they had never set eyes on a white man before. Then he realized there was more to it. They weren't just staring. The only word he could think of to describe their expressions was "hopeful," but that made no damn sense.

"This is my grandfather, Broken Horn," Swift Fox said. "My parents were slain by Piegans when I was young and he took me in."

"What about all these others?"

"Family and friends. They always come with me when I enter a race. A lone Indian woman in a white town is never safe."

She had a point, Fargo conceded. Too many whites were like Spike Yokum. They looked down their noses at anyone with red skin. To them, Indians were little better than animals. Yet that didn't stop them from raping Indian women if they thought they could get away with it.

Broken Horn had stooped to enter the largest lodge. Swift Fox held the flap for Fargo and said, "After you."

Lodge etiquette required that Fargo step to the right and wait for his host to seat him. Buffalo Horn sat cross-legged at the rear, on the far side of a small fire, then beckoned for Fargo to take the place of honor on his left. One by one other Crows filed in, until soon most of the band had assembled.

Fargo knew better than to ask why he had been invited. It would be considered rude. He had to be patient. Eventually they would get around to telling him.

The women passed food around. They had whipped up a feast, further proof there was more to the occasion than a casual get-together. Fargo was given a large tin plate heaped with stewed venison. His side dishes consisted of a boiled pudding made with dried berries and flour, fried roots, and sweet cakes. To wash it down he was allowed all the piping hot coffee he could drink.

Little was said during the meal. The women sat off by themselves with the children, as was the custom, with a notable exception. Swift Fox was seated at her grandfather's right elbow, which was unheard of. Fargo learned why when the meal was over and the warriors were filling and lighting their pipes.

"My grandfather has asked me to translate. He knows you are versed in sign talk, but he wants to be sure you understand how important this is to our band and our people."

"I'm all ears." Fargo leaned back. After gorging himself, he was in no great hurry to return to town. Besides, he would like to get to know Swift Fox better. A *lot* better.

"We wish to discuss the race. The prize is important to us. My people have grown to depend on me and I would not let them down if I could help it."

"No one can predict who will win."

"True. All I ask is a fair chance. But look at what

happened to the Englishman, and the attempt on Amarillo's life. Someone is out to harm the fastest runners, and I do not want to be next."

"Odds are they won't hurt a woman," Fargo observed. The fairer gender was held in high esteem on the frontier, in large part because the ratio of males to females was on the order of ten to one.

"A white woman, perhaps. But we both know a red woman is not treated with the same respect. Whoever tried to kill the Apache might try to do the same to me."

Broken Horn interrupted. He went on for quite a while in their tongue. When he was done he sat back, puffing on his pipe.

Swift Fox cleared her throat. "My grandfather thanks you again for coming. He says he has heard much about you, how you always speak with a straight tongue, how you have lived among our kind, and are fair in all your dealings."

Fargo smiled at his host to be polite. Inwardly, he wondered where all this was leading. The Crows wanted something, something big, or they wouldn't be going to all this trouble.

"Since you have lived as we do, you know firsthand the cycles of our lives. How a tribe has full bellies in the summer and lean times in the winter. How we live from hand to mouth, as your people would say. At times it can be a hard life but we never complain. It is our lot and we accept it."

Fargo could see this was going to take a while. He held out his empty cup and one of the women filled it.

"Every member of our tribe must do what they can for the good of all. When our warriors go on a buffalo surround, they must work as a group and stalk the herd alone or they might spook it, and everyone will go hungry. When a woman finds a large patch of ripe berries or roots, she must not hoard them for her own family, but should share the news so all can enjoy in the bounty."

"Many tribes live that way," Fargo mentioned. They had to. The constant threat of starvation was the midwife to cooperation.

"True. We are no different. But we have learned to do something many tribes have not. We have learned how to use white ways to our advantage." Swift Fox ran a hand across her hair to keep it out of her eyes. "Take that which you call money. To a Blood or a Pawnee it is of no value. Nothing but meaningless bits of metal and pieces of paper. They have not yet learned that in the white world, money is the key to everything."

"But the Crows have?"

"The money I win goes for food, clothes and tools for my people. I do not keep it for myself." Swift Fox motioned. "Surely you have noticed the many white items we possess?"

Now that she brought it up, Fargo had noticed an unusual amount, everything from cooking utensils to spoons and forks, from belts and knives and axes to blankets and a few store-bought shirts.

"More prize money is being offered for this one race than for all the others I have entered combined. Enough so that our band will never want for anything ever again. Enough to last us to the end of our days."

"Good luck," Fargo said.

"I need more than that. My people need more than that. We need assurances I will not be hurt." Swift Fox looked expectantly at him. "Assurances only you can give."

"Me?" Fargo sat up. "I don't have a say in things. The town council is running the event. They make the rules. Talk to them."

"It is not the rules I worry about. So long as they are applied fairly, what more can anyone ask?" Swift Fox grew pensive. "I do not want to die. Death holds no fear for me, but failing my people does. They have grown to depend on the money I win for the many things it can buy."

In Fargo's opinion they were making a mistake. Time and again he had seen tribes try to be like the white man, only to lose the values and traditions that made them a tribe to begin with. "I still don't see how I can be of any help."

"We have heard how you hire out to the blue coats to scout for them, and how you earn money as a tracker." Swift Fox glanced at her grandfather, who produced a buckskin purse from under his shirt and gave it to her. "My people would like to hire you to serve as my protector."

Fargo looked from her to her grandfather and back again. They were serious. Momentarily at a loss what to say, he feigned interest in his coffee.

"We apologize for not knowing the customary amount to offer." Swift Fox jangled the purse. "Is three hundred dollars enough? It would only be for one day. Once the race is over, your obligation is over."

"That's a lot of money." More than Fargo earned in two weeks of army work. "But my gun isn't for hire. You said it yourself. I scout, I track, I blaze trails. I wouldn't be right for the job."

"I can think of no one better qualified. Your courage is well known. So is your skill with a revolver and rifle. What more does a protector need?"

Fargo cut right to the core. "I don't want your life on my hands. If something happened to you, I'd never forgive myself."

A pink tinge suffused Swift Fox's cheeks. "I thank you for your honesty. But whether you agree to help or not, my life is still at risk. They have already tried once to kill me."

Fargo was taken aback. "When?"

"This morning. Shortly after I woke up, I opened the flap to go to the spring for water, as I usually do." Rising, Swift Fox walked to the front of the lodge and touched her finger to a small hole. "There was a shot. A bullet missed me and almost hit my grandmother."

"Did you see who did it?"

"No. I closed the flap and dropped to the ground. Buffalo Horn and the other warriors armed themselves and conducted a search. They found the tracks of a white man and his horse."

Sent by Yokum or Quinby? Fargo wondered. So far all the top runners except Luther Samuels had been attacked. Although for all he knew, Samuels had, too. He should look the hothead up when he got back to Nugget.

Swift Fox reclaimed her spot and placed the poke between them. "What do you say? Will you guard me until the race is over?"

Fargo wanted to help. He truly did.

"We have another twenty-five dollars if this is not enough. It is all we have left, I am afraid."

Buffalo Horn had been puffing contentedly on his long-stemmed pipe. Now he lowered it and addressed Fargo for over a minute. Once again Swift Fox translated. "Hear me, He-Who-Tracks. We ask you to do this not just for the money. The food and blankets and clothes it buys are nice, but my granddaughter's life is more important. We want her safe. I have tried to convince her not to run but she will not listen. She is stubborn like her mother, my daughter, and thinks she knows better than those who have lived many winters more than she."

Fargo disliked being put on the spot. "You honor me with your trust," he chose his words carefully, "but Swift Fox isn't the only runner in danger. I can be of better help watching over all of them."

"You would do that for people you hardly know?"

"I have a personal stake. My own life has been threatened." And if there was one thing Fargo never stood for, it was that. Back east threats were often bluster, hot air spewed by those who lacked the will and the means to carry them out. Not so west of the Mississippi, where gunplay was as routine as breathing and cemeteries were filled with the bones of those who didn't take their enemies seriously enough.

Swift Fox and her grandfather were huddled shoulder to shoulder. The old warrior grunted a few times, then shifted. "When you say you will watch over the runners, does this include my granddaughter?"

"When I say all, I mean all." Fargo wasn't fooling himself. It would be next to impossible for one man to cover the entire race from start to finish. Which was why he said, "But I can't do it alone. Your own warriors can help. Post them at spots where an ambush is likely and be on the lookout for whites with rifles."

Buffalo Horn scowled and responded through his granddaughter, "Am I to understand you would have us take up arms against white men?"

"For Swift Fox's sake, yes."

The old Crow's scowl deepened. "I love her as if she were my own child, but you ask too much. If we kill a white man, it would bring the blue coats down on our heads."

"Not if I speak up for you," Fargo offered. "Not if I tell them it was my idea."

Silence filled the tepee. Warriors shifted and looked at one another. Women held their children closer. Buffalo Horn set his pipe down and somberly related, "You mean well, He-Who-Tracks. But your request is ill-advised. When a white man kills an Indian, other whites do nothing. When an Indian kills a white man, many other Indians suffer."

Fargo began to speak but the old warrior held up a hand.

"Many winters have I lived. Much have I seen in my time. When Little Bear stole a horse from a white trapper, the trapper and five friends hunted Little

Bear down and shot him. They also shot his woman when she tried to stop them, burned down his lodge, took all Little Bear's horses, and left his head on a pole as a warning."

"That was years ago," Fargo said, but the Crow leader wasn't done.

"When Pawnees killed and scalped a white man, their village was destroyed. When Sioux attacked white wagons, blue coats drove them from their village and chased them to the land of geysers. When the Cheyenne stole a white woman, the whites did not rest until they recovered her. Eighty Cheyenne were slain." Buffalo Horn raised his head. "The meaning is clear. Harm one white, and many suffer. Your kind are like grizzlies. When they are mad, they do not stop until they have destroyed that which made them mad."

Arguing would get Fargo nowhere. Not when it was all true. "So I gather you won't help watch over the runners tomorrow? I respect your view, Broken Horn. You must do what you feel is best for your people. Just as I must do what is best for the runners."

"I understand. All I ask is that when you do, you watch my granddaughter more closely than the rest."

Fargo uncrossed his legs. Staying longer was pointless. "I must be getting back. I thank you for your hospitality and hope we can do this again sometime." As many frowns as smiles followed him to the opening.

Night had fallen, dominated by a quarter moon, and stars lavishly sprinkled the firmament. Fargo was only a few strides from the Ovaro when a hand fell on his shoulder.

"You left so quickly I could not thank you for coming," Swift Fox said. "Some of the others do not understand but I harbor no ill feelings.'

Fargo touched a fingertip to Swift Fox's chin. "Just do me a favor. Keep your eyes skinned tomorrow. I'd hate for anything to happen to someone as beautiful as you."

The compliment seemed to go unnoticed. "You would be wise to heed your own advice," Swift Fox said. "There are rumors you have made powerful enemies, and I would not like it if anything happened to someone as handsome as you."

Fargo couldn't say whether she was sincere or being sarcastic. Stepping into the stirrups, he reined toward town. "Until tomorrow."

A cool breeze fanned his face as he tapped his spurs against the Ovaro. Absorbed in thought, he had gone half a mile when off in the darkness a hoof scraped on stone. Swiveling in the saddle, he sought the source but saw nothing to account for it. There was always the chance his nerves were on edge. But to be on the safe side, once he was past the next bend, he veered into the shadows and drew rein.

Minutes elapsed but no one appeared. No sounds broke the benighted stillness. Fargo rode on, looking back every now and again. He speculated whether it might be a Crow sent to ensure he made it back. Or maybe it was Swift Fox. He would like nothing more than to be alone with her a while, but it was wishful thinking on his part. Her last comment notwithstanding, she wouldn't venture from the Crow camp this late.

Fargo had gone a couple of hundred yards when he glanced to the south and spied the silhouette of another rider. He continued on as if he hadn't noticed, watching closely from under his hat brim. He couldn't tell much in the dark but he suspected it was a white man from the way the man sat the saddle. Had the rider been there all along? Had he been followed all the way from town and not realized it? If it was an assassin out to ambush him, why hadn't the killer struck yet? So many questions, and only one way to get the answers.

Ahead, the trail wound past a low bluff that would

temporarily conceal him. Fargo bided his time, and as soon as he was in the bluff's shadow, he reined up. With any luck, the rider would go a short distance before becoming aware that something was amiss.

Counting to ten in his head, Fargo wheeled the Ovaro and retraced its steps, bending low so he was less likely to be spotted. Forty yards out he reined to the south. It would take him less than a minute to reach the higher ground at a full gallop but the racket would alert the bushwhacker. So he held to a walk, his right hand on his Colt.

The rider hadn't reappeared. Fargo scowled every time the Ovaro's hooves clattered on hard rock, but it couldn't be helped. He was almost to the spot where he had last seen the rider when he straightened. A rifle cracked and a hornet buzzed his ear. He saw the flash, whipped out his Colt, and answered in kind. Two shots. Fired so swiftly they echoed like one.

Hooves hammered. Fargo glimpsed the rider, racing toward Nugget. He gave chase, letting the Ovaro have its head. Whoever he was after owned a good horse; he wasn't able to gain no matter how he tried.

In due course Nugget's lights sparkled like fireflies, and the rider made the mistake of looking back. Fargo registered a bearded face under a short-crowned dark hat. Wisely, the killer avoided the well-lit main streets and guided his mount into a dark alley. Fargo was only twenty seconds behind him but that was too much. When he came to the other end, the rider had melted into Nugget's bustling nightlife.

Fargo glanced right and left and saw a dozen scattered men on horseback. Any could be the one he was after. Or maybe the killer had ducked into an alley across the street.

Leaning against a post a few yards away was a fallen dove, her dress as revealing as the sheerest of nightgowns. She winked and smiled. "Looking for a good time, handsome?"

"I'm looking for a man who came through here before me. Any chance you saw which way he went?"

Her grin widened. "I might have. Provided there's a chance you have five dollars to spare."

Fargo produced the money. "I'll be back if you lie to me."

The dove laughed. "Why would I? He means nothing to me." She pointed. "See that saloon a block or so down? His horse is at the rail."

Touching his hat brim, Fargo moved into the middle of the street. No one was in front of the saloon, nor was anyone looking out. Of the eight horses out front, a sorrel on the far end was lathered with sweat, its head bent in exhaustion. Dismounting next to it, Fargo loosened the Colt in its holster.

Some saloons were grand establishments with polished bars and glittering chandeliers. Others, like this one, had dirt floors and a long plank held up by upended barrels for a bar. The customers were as rough and aloof as the place itself, and many a suspicious eye was fixed in Fargo's direction. Sliding to the left so his back was to the wall, Fargo studied every customer. Over half had beards. Those who were unarmed he discounted right away. That left nine or ten, sprinkled at random throughout the room. He concentrated on those at the bar.

Bent over the plank as if trying to be inconspicuous was a thin man in grimy range clothes and badly scuffed boots. He had his head turned the other way but an unkempt beard was visible.

Gliding along the wall, Fargo called out, "You there! With the blue bandanna! Turn around, bushwhacker!"

All talk ceased.

Those nearest the gunman backed away. The bartender looked as if he were going to say something but changed his mind.

The man hadn't moved.

"You heard me!" Fargo snapped. "Let's see you take a shot at me now."

Slowly straightening, the assassin turned. His elbows were on the plank, his hands nowhere near his gun belt. "Are you talkin' to me, mister?" Ferret eyes danced with resentment as his mouth curled in a sneer over rodent teeth. "I don't have any idea what in hell you're talkin' about."

"Who sent you to kill me?"

"Are you hard of hearin'?" the man rejoined. "I've never set eyes on you until this very moment. Go make a nuisance of yourself somewhere else."

Fargo was positive he had the right man. "Nice try, but I wasn't born yesterday. You have two choices. Guess what they are? Be sure you choose the right one."

"Oh, I think I have more than that." The gunman lowered his arms to his sides. "And the one I like best is where my pards and I turn you into coyote bait."

Pards? Fargo heard chairs scrape. Three poker players had risen and were spreading out. It had never occurred to him the assassin might have come here to meet with friends.

"Now then," the gunman smugly declared. "You have one choice, and one choice only. Guess what it is?"

8

Skye Fargo knew his limitations. He was quick on the draw, but he wasn't fast enough to drop all four gunmen before they put some slugs in him. His best bet was to dive for the floor as he drew and hope to heaven they were rotten shots.

The rodent at the bar was enjoying himself. "Cat got your tongue, mister? You were all set to buck me out in gore a minute ago. But now you're not talkin' so big, are you?"

Fargo was boxed in. He couldn't make it to the door if he wanted to. The other customers were all on their feet, pressing back against the walls to avoid taking a stray bullet.

"This turned out a lot easier than I was told it would be," the rodent declared. "Tricking you into comin' in here was like takin' honey from a baby."

Fargo wanted to kick himself for walking into their trap. But first he had to make it out alive. He studied the other three hard cases, trying to decide which was deadliest. One wore his hog leg tied down low. Another had his revolver wedged under his belt rather than in a holster.

The tension was thick enough to cut with a dull scythe. No one showed any interest in helping even the odds. They were holding their collective breath, waiting for the blasts of lead and flame.

It was then that low laughter filled the room. Mirth

as cold as the ice that crowned the mountains in December, and as hard as the rock that mantled them in July.

When the gunmen glanced toward the entrance Fargo risked a look, too.

Things had just gone from terribly bad to vastly worse.

Just inside the door stood Silvermane, his thumbs hooked on either side of his belt buckle. Lamp light gleamed off the pearl handles of his matched set of Smith and Wessons. His grin was reminiscent of a cat about to pounce on a caged canary. "Well, well. What have we here?"

Figuring Silvermane was in league with the other gunmen, Fargo turned. When it came to being deadly, the small shootist in black was in a class by himself. "So this was your doing."

"Me?" Silvermane laughed again. "Your family wasn't big on brains, were they? I'm here to help you, not plant you."

The amazement that washed over Fargo was mirrored by the rodent at the bar and his three partners. "Since when do you care if I'm shot to pieces? I thought you wanted me dead."

"I do," Silvermane asserted. "But *I* want to be the one to do it." He regarded the four gunnies. "As for these peckerwoods, they work for someone else."

The rodent had lost a lot of his bluster. "What the hell is going on here? This doesn't concern you, Silvermane."

"You couldn't be more wrong, Wharton. I'm under orders not to let anyone throw down on this lunkhead, and the only way to be sure you don't is to do to you as you and your pards were fixing to do to him." The small man in black spread his legs a trifle more, setting himself. "Whenever you hombres are ready to have your flames snuffed out, try your best."

The four gunmen didn't like it, they didn't like it

one bit, but if nothing else flattering could be said of them, they weren't cowards. Two faced off against Silvermane. That left Wharton and another for Fargo.

"I'll kill my two and work on over," Silvermane said to him as if it would be the simplest feat in the world.

"I don't need any help," Fargo responded curtly. The small gunfighter had a knack for getting under his skin.

"Sure you don't. It would serve you right if I left." But Silvermane stayed where he was, and nodded at Wharton. "What are you waiting for? Quinby to come to your rescue? It wouldn't change anything. I don't answer to him. When all is said and done, men like us can't rely on anyone."

"You've got that right." Wharton nervously licked his lips. The odds were not to his liking but he went for his revolver anyway, his hand a blur, his draw the signal for the others.

Fargo saw the muzzle of Wharton's pistol rise toward him but he had the Colt out and up, and he fired first. Shifting, he banged off a shot at the gunman who wore a strapped-down hog leg. Both killers were jolted in their tracks but only the second one crashed to the floor.

Wharton triggered a round that plowed a furrow in the dirt floor. Fargo instantly squeezed off two more shots and the rodent staggered against the bar. Mouth agape, Wharton desperately tried to fire again but limp fingers betrayed him. He slid down, gasped once, and gave up the ghost.

Instantly, Fargo spun. Silvermane had disposed of the other two and swung toward him. They stared at one another through swirling gunsmoke until the small man in black twirled his Smith and Wessons into his silver-studded holsters.

"As much as I'd like it to be, now isn't the time."

Wary of a ruse, Fargo reloaded. The patrons remained packed against the walls, not entirely convinced it was over.

"When you're ready, my boss would like a few words with you. He's waiting for us at the Motherlode."

"I have nothing to say to him."

Silvermane indicated a still twitching form. "I did you a favor. The least you can do is hear Mr. Yokum out. He's the one who told me to be damn sure you don't come to any harm."

"What does he care?"

"You'd have to ask him. I'm the hired help. He doesn't always take me into his confidence."

"All I want is his promise not to go after the runners." Fargo was going after the mayor. A reckoning was due. First there had been the rifleman who tried to kill Amarillo, now Wharton.

"You have to talk to Mr. Yokum in person," Silvermane persisted. "I can't make promises for him."

Fargo decided a short delay was worth it if it helped put an end to the bloodshed. "After you."

"Can I trust you not to drill me in the back?" The man in black laughed and swaggered out, where another crowd had collected. They gave the bantam rooster a wide berth, pushing one another in their frantic haste to get out of his way.

"Can you smell it, Fargo?" Silvermane asked.

"Smell what?"

"Their fear. The fear men like us inspire in sheep like them." Silvermane pushed a man who didn't move fast enough. "Maybe rabbits is more like it. Timid, cowardly little rabbits who wouldn't last two seconds against either of us. They live their whole lives scared. Afraid of this, afraid of that, but mainly afraid of the grave men like you and I put them in if they don't show us the proper respect."

"Speak for yourself." Fargo's dislike of the gunfighter climbed. He had met men like Silvermane before. They reveled in the power their ability with a six-shooter gave them. It had an intoxicating effect, like whiskey or opium, and they couldn't get enough.

"Are you going to tell me you've never gotten fed up with the rabbits of this world?" Silvermane queried. "Hasn't there ever been a time you've wanted to blow some idiot's brains out for breathing the same air you do?"

"I don't kill for killing's sake."

Silvermane paused. "There's pleasure in killing whether you're willing to admit it or not. Me, I'll put windows in anyone's skull for the sheer fun of it."

Fargo was silent until they reached the Motherlode. He had to wade through a solid press of people to reach the far table occupied by Spike Yokum and four poker players. A fifth chair was empty.

Spike patted it and smiled. "I've been saving this for you, Mr. Fargo. We have a lot to talk about, you and I. Issues of great importance to both of us."

Pulling the chair out, Fargo eased down. Something about Yokum's greeting bothered him. Yokum had the look of a man who held all the trump cards and couldn't wait to play his hand. "Make it quick. I have someone to see."

Silvermane had bent and was whispering in his employer's ear. Yokum's smile grew. "Would you excuse us, gentlemen?" he said to the other players. "We can continue this game another time. My friend and I need to be alone."

"I'm hardly your friend," Fargo commented as the men collected their stakes and rose. Not one had objected.

"Now then," Yokum began, "my associate has informed me of the gunplay down the street. It must gall you, him bailing you out of a tight situation like that. I daresay you're fit to be tied."

Yokum's smile irritated Fargo no end. "Get to the point."

"Really now. Is it too much to ask for you to be civil? Our arrangement need not be conducted on sour terms."

"What the hell are you talking about?" Fargo was about ready to walk out. "We don't have any *arrangement*."

"Not yet. But we will soon enough. You are going to help me out, just as Silvermane helped you." Yokum finally stopped smiling. "Whether you want to or not."

Fargo started to rise. He'd had enough.

"Rushing off to see the charming Miss Endelstrom, are you? She could prove hard to find. I happen to know where she is, but I'll only tell you if you listen to my proposal."

Fargo didn't like the sound of that. Reluctantly, he sat back down.

"Thank you." Yokum practically dripped sarcasm. "As you know, I find myself in an unpleasant situation. My rivalry with the mayor is common knowledge, and I refuse to let that sniveling pig get the better of me in the upcoming footrace." Yokum paused. "But you've heard all this before."

Anger simmered in Fargo like boiling water in a pot. "Get to the damn point."

"My point has to do with the whims of fate. All the trouble Quinby and I went to, all the time it took to contact Sherwood and Thorne and the cost of paying their travel expenses, and all for what? Now neither can take part tomorrow." Yokum fiddled with his cards. "I was content to let matters rest. So long as Quinby isn't backing a runner, I couldn't care less who wins. But now he's gone and complicated things again in a way that has a direct bearing on you."

"I don't see how."

"Word reached me earlier that our illustrious mayor has found another runner, and if his new man wins, Quinby will gloat up a storm." Yokum crumpled one of the cards and flung it at the wall. "I can't allow that."

Fargo had to ask. "Who did Quinby find to replace the earl? I thought it was too late for new runners to enter."

"It is. Whether in person or by proxy, the deadline was five days ago." Yokum grinned and winked. "So there would be plenty of time for bets to be placed at my establishment and others. Bets on which a slight fee is paid. Fees that add up quite nicely."

"Who?" Fargo prodded when the name wasn't forthcoming.

"Luther Samuels. The mayor promised him an additional thousand dollars should Samuels win." Yokum's features clouded. "The fool. Quinby was willing to pay Sherwood Desmond five thousand."

Fargo still didn't see where any of this had anything to do with him. So what if Quinby had found another runner? He voiced the question aloud.

"Have you been listening to a word I've said?" Yokum balled his fists. "I refuse to let Quinby get the better of me. *Ever.* I hate the man, Mr. Fargo. I despise him. Loathe him. So I will do all in my considerable power to thwart Luther Samuels."

The solution, as Fargo saw it, was simple enough. "Get your own runner."

"Now why didn't I think of that?" Yokum chuckled. "But who to chose? It has to be someone with a real chance at beating Samuels. The Apache is good but I wouldn't trust him any further than I can throw the bar. The Crow girl is exceptional, but when I sent one of my men to make a polite inquiry, she made it abundantly plain she would rather be staked out on an anthill than have anything to do with me."

"I don't blame her."

The verbal parry rolled off Yokum like water off a

duck's back. "So there I was. In dire need but with no one I could count on. Then I recalled hearing about an incident the day you arrived. It seems you thought Sherwood, Samuels and Amarillo were after Swift Fox, and you gallantly rushed to her rescue."

"So?"

"So it's my understanding you overtook the three of them *on foot*. That you chased them down and caught them." Yokum shifted his chair and studied Fargo more closely. "I must admit, you certainly are a fit physical specimen. Your stamina must be extraordinary."

Fargo didn't like where their talk was leading. "You can't be thinking what I think you're thinking."

"Why not? It's rumored you have lived among Indians. That you're as tough as rawhide, as quick as lightning. Who better to run the race for me than you?"

"You're loco," Fargo declared. "It's ten miles long. I wouldn't last half that."

"Tsk, tsk. You think a lot less of your ability than I do. With the right incentive, I believe you can go the distance. In fact, properly motivated, I believe you have a very real chance of being the victor."

"There's nothing you can say or do that would convince me to run for you," Fargo flatly stated.

Yokum's eyes glittered like a serpent's. "Sadly, you're mistaken. One word will suffice. One word will ensure you do exactly as I require."

Fargo suppressed an urge to punch him in the mouth. "And what word would that be?"

"Marta."

Fargo gazed toward the street in alarm. Once again he began to push up out of his chair.

"I'm afraid you won't find her at her place of employment," Yokum quickly said. "You see, I took the liberty of making the young woman's acquaintance earlier this evening while you were off visiting the Crows."

Forgetting himself, Fargo grabbed Yokum by the shirt. "If you've hurt her, you bastard!"

Yokum didn't lift a finger to defend himself. "Assaulting me will do you no good. The young woman is my guest. Rest assured, I haven't harmed a hair on her pretty head. Why should I, when she is a means to a marvelous end?" He motioned. "Please. Sit down and we'll discuss this rationally."

His emotions in upheaval, Fargo stepped back. He'd rather beat Yokum to a pulp but he didn't dare with Marta in his clutches. Silvermane and several other gunmen were grinning at his expense, another insult he had to swallow. For the time being.

"That's better," Yokum coaxed, as if he were dealing with a five-year old. "Now here's how it's going to be. You will run the race for me. Not only that, you will win by any and every means necessary. Any questions?"

"You're forgetting something, aren't you?" Fargo clutched at a straw. "No new runners are allowed to enter. You said so yourself."

"Ah. True enough. But there is a clause that permits substitutions. If a runner bows out for any reason, he or she may pick an alternate to run in their place. It's a concession we made when we drew up the rules since the entry fee is nonrefundable." Yokum waited a moment before dropping the other shoe. "Richard Thorne, at my request, has selected you as his alternate."

"Quinby won't stand for it."

"He has no choice. It's perfectly legitimate. He would have done the same except no one else locally is up to the challenge. So he picked someone who had already entered."

Fargo could barely contain his rage. Yokum had him backed into a corner. With Marta's life at stake, refusing wasn't an option. "What if I do my best and still lose?"

"I'm not a charitable man, but I'm not unreasonable, either. If, in my estimation, you have given your utmost but someone else wins, I will release Marta to you unharmed." Yokum leaned forward. "Just so it's clear, the only one I care about is Samuels. He mustn't win. Quinby mustn't win. Anyone else is fine, *just not Samuels.*"

Seldom had Fargo yearned to put a slug into someone as much as he did at that moment.

"If looks could kill, Mr. Fargo, I daresay I'd be lying on this floor as cold as mountain snow. But keep this in mind. Should anything happen to me, I've arranged it so Miss Endelstrom's life is forfeit. Most of my men have compunctions about hurting a woman, but there is one on my payroll capable of eliminating anyone, anytime."

Fargo glanced at the small man in black. "Let me guess."

"Casting stones ill becomes you. By all accounts, you've slain almost as many, if not more, than he has."

"I never kill for blood money."

Yokum shrugged. "Killing is killing. The excuse is irrelevant." He spread his hands out on the table. "Be that as it may, I suggest you concentrate all your energies on the race."

"Tell me more about it." Fargo might as well find out what he was letting himself in for.

"You've been to the starting point outside of town? From there the course is clearly marked. It loops around and ends at a grandstand constructed especially for the occasion on the south edge of Nugget. There will be a band, food booths, pony rides for the kids, everything."

"You know where you can stuff your pony rides."

Yokum clucked a few times. "Honestly, now. This hostility is misdirected. Try to look at the bright side."

"There is one?"

Silvermane cackled but nipped his laughter when Yokum gave him a sharp look. "Yes, Mr. Fargo, there most definitely is. Should you win, you not only keep the ten thousand in prize money, I will add another five to the pot to repay you for your efforts."

Men like Spike Yocum were all the same. They thought money was the answer to everything. It was their god, their lifeblood, and they thought everyone else was the same. Fargo intended to prove differently once the race was over and Marta was safe.

"Before you go, I hope you will indulge me." Yokum snapped his fingers. From behind the bar came the bartender carrying a tray. But he wasn't bringing drinks. On the tray were a pair of shoes, which he set on the card table in front of Fargo. "Try them on. They're Mr. Thorne's, but your feet are about his size. Thorne swears they're the most comfortable running shoes he's ever worn."

Fargo picked one up. It was constructed of calfskin, the leather soft and pliable. Ankle high, it had a dozen tiny eyelets, and grooves in the thin sole. For better traction, he guessed.

"All the best runners wear them," Yokum remarked. "The Englishmen has a pair but his feet are much too small."

Fargo stood. "Remind me, what time does the race start?"

"Ten o'clock. Mayor Quinby will give a short speech beforehand." Yokum's eyes narrowed. "We are in agreement, then? You will run for me?" He extended his right hand. "Let's shake on it, shall we?"

"Go to hell."

Yokum frowned. "Fair enough. If that's how you want to be, it's your prerogative. But I'd hoped we could conduct this on an adult basis." He wagged a finger at Silvermane and another gunman. "My associates will go with you and take turns standing guard throughout the night. From a discreet distance, of course."

"I don't need a baby-sitter." Fargo grabbed the special shoes.

"Mayor Quinby has already made one attempt on your life. I wouldn't put it past him to try again. He has ears everywhere, and he's bound to learn I have enlisted your services."

Silvermane strutted up. "Don't you fret none, big man. I won't let anyone harm a hair on your slow-as-molasses head."

A red haze filled Fargo's eyes. He came within a whisker of drawing but was able to bottle his fury. Without another word he plowed toward the doors, not caring who he shouldered aside. The crisp night air was like a splash of cold water in the face, and he stood gulping it in.

"Is it true?"

The question came out of nowhere. Fargo turned to his left and beheld Nugget's second leading sidewinder, flanked by Marshal Darnell.

"Is it true?" Mayor Quinby repeated. "Word has reached me that my nemesis plans to ask you to run on his behalf."

Fargo glanced into the saloon. The only way the mayor could have heard was if he had spies paid to eavesdrop, or if one of the gunmen on Yokum's payroll was also on Quinby's.

Silvermane moved between them, his thumbs hooked in his silver-studded gun belt, as usual. "What if it is? There's not a damn thing you can do about it. If you don't believe me, take it up with Mr. Yokum."

"Watch your tone," Quinby upbraided him.

"Or what? You'll sic your puppy on me?" Silvermane sneered at the lawman. "Hell, he couldn't outdraw me if both my wrists were tied."

Marshal Darnell wasn't a complete fool. He didn't let his dander get up.

Mayor Quinby had more grit. "One of these days

you'll get yours, gunfighter. Everyone meets someone faster eventually."

"Maybe so," Silvermane said, "but if I have any say, and I do, it won't be for a good long while." He placed his hands on the pearl grips of his revolvers. "You're welcome to try, though, either of you." When neither took him up on it, he laughed and said to Fargo, "Let's go. The boss told me you're spending the night at your girlfriend's. We've got her stashed away so you'll have her place all to yourself."

The walk there was a blur. Fargo's temples were pounding like a blacksmith's hammer, and molten fire flowed in his veins. He was a keg of black powder on the verge of exploding. For Marta's sake he had to keep it all inside. He had to bottle up his outrage and his humiliation and not let it out until the right moment.

Then they would pay.

Oh, *how* they would pay!

Spike Yokum and Silvermane and Mayor Quinby and Marshal Darnell didn't know it yet, but their day of reckoning was near.

9

Close to a thousand people were on hand for the big event, some from as far away as San Francisco and Salt Lake City. One party of thirty had traveled from distant Kansas City, sporting men who never passed up an opportunity to indulge their pet passion. Hawkers were out by the score, selling everything from parasols and sausages to special flyers Mayor Quinby had printed to commemorate the occasion. Cups of water went for five cents and the vendors couldn't keep up with demand.

By ten o'clock the temperature pushed eighty. Many of the ladies wore hats with rims as wide as sombreros to ward off the sun. Women and men fanned themselves with folded newspapers and the like. Kids raced wildly about, laughing and playing, as oblivious to the heat as they were to the urging of their parents to behave.

Fargo took all this in as he rode up to the starting area and dismounted. He was among the last runners to arrive. The others were flexing their legs and going through all sorts of contortions in preparation. He saw Swift Fox. She smiled and nodded and he returned the favor.

Silvermane and a pair of lanky gunmen reined up. They had been waiting when Fargo emerged from Marta's apartment and had accompanied him "for his own protection," as the gunfighter phrased it.

"Are you going to run in the race with me, too?" Fargo quipped as he opened his saddlebags and removed the special shoes.

"I draw the line at giving myself heat stroke." Silvermane rested his hands on his saddle horn. "This is where we part company for a spell. The boss reckons Quinby wouldn't dare have you shot while the race is in progress. It'd cause too much of a stink. So, you're on your own."

"And Marta?"

"You get to see her when the race is over and not before. That's the deal, remember?" Silvermane grinned. "I have ten dollars riding on you so don't let me down, you hear?"

Sitting, Fargo set to work removing his spurs and boots. "By the way, I haven't seen Mitch around. Is he the one watching over Marta?"

"Good hunch," the gunfighter responded. "Don't worry. He's under orders not to lay a finger on her or he'll answer to Mr. Yokum. Your girlfriend is fine. Hold up your end of the bargain and she'll stay that way."

Fargo smiled. Another name to add to the list. "Shouldn't you go play with the other brats?"

Silvermane leaned down. "When the stupid race is over we're finishing this. I'll be generous and let you pick the time and place. But only one of us will ever leave this two-bit town."

"I wouldn't have it any other way." Fargo unfastened the ankle sheath of his Arkansas Toothpick and slid the knife into his left boot. He pulled on the calfskin shoes. The night before he had tried them out and they fit comfortably enough, but they felt strange after so many years of wearing boots. He laced the shoes and pushed to his feet.

Silvermane and the gunhands were gone. In their place was someone else. "So it's true. I couldn't believe it when the mayor told me you were runnin' for a piece of scum like Spike Yokum." Luther Samuels hitched at his overalls.

"You're a fine one to talk," Fargo dryly replied as he turned to shove his boots, spurs and knife into a saddlebag.

"What's that crack supposed to mean?" the black man demanded.

"You're running for Quinby and he's no better than Yokum." Fargo tried to close the flap but the saddlebag was too full.

"How can you compare them? The mayor is a nice enough fella for a politician. Yokum, on the other hand, has a pack of hired killers at his beck and call. It's like mixin' polecats and puppies."

"You honestly don't know, do you?"

"Know what?" Samuels was wearing the same floppy hat, pulled low against the sun's glare.

"Never mind." Fargo was in no mood for a long-winded explanation. "Just don't hold it against me if I win."

Samuels chortled with glee. "That'll be the day. I'm one of the fastest critters on two legs, and I can go all day and all night without tirin'. You might as well kiss that prize money so long."

Off to one side stood Amarillo, everyone giving him a wide berth. He glanced at Fargo and Fargo nodded but the Mimbre didn't acknowledge it.

"I need this money, need it bad," Samuels went on. "Need it more than any of you, and that's a fact."

"So you said before," Fargo noted. "Mind telling me why?"

The black man hesitated, then shrugged. "I guess it can't hurt." A dreamy expression came over him. "It's my sweetheart, Esmerelda. She and I want to be man and wife but her owner won't set her free. He claims she's too valuable. But hellfire, she's just one of two hundred slaves he's got on that plantation of his." His temper ever mercurial, Samuels smashed his right fist against his left palm. "He said I could have her if I came up with enough money. Three thousand dollars! He set the amount high figurin' I wouldn't be able to. But I'll teach him! I'll have enough to set her free and then some!"

"Good luck," Fargo said.

"I don't need luck when I've got these." Samuels smacked his legs and hopped up and down a few times. "You watch. All these crackers will be eatin' my dust before this is done." He moved off among the milling runners.

Fargo was about to do likewise when a man in a suit and stovepipe hat approached. Affixed to his jacket was a yellow rectangle that read RACE OFFICIAL. Under his arm was a black satchel. "Pardon me. Are you running today?"

"Would I be wearing these stupid shoes if I wasn't?"

The official pointed at Fargo's waist. "I'm sorry, sir, but the wearing of firearms by participants is expressly forbidden. You'll have to leave your pistol here."

Sure enough, Fargo surveyed the runners, and not one had a weapon. Still, the prospect of being unarmed didn't appeal to him. "I don't want my Colt stolen."

"It won't be. The organizers have thought of everything." The official pointed again, this time at two townsmen with shotguns who were strolling along the uneven line of horses. "Their job is to guard the mounts and valuables of everyone taking part in the race."

Against his better judgement Fargo unstrapped his Colt, rolled up the gun belt, and crammed them into his other saddlebag.

"One more thing." The official opened his satchel and held out a bright pink ribbon. "Here."

"What the hell is this for?"

"All runners are required to wear them so the monitors can determine who is a runner and who isn't."

Only then did Fargo realize other officials were roving about passing out ribbons to those who needed them. "Do we wear them in our hair?" he snapped.

"Please, sir." The man wagged the ribbon. "It's required. If you would like to lodge a protest, you're certainly welcome to take it up with the oversight committee. But I'm afraid it wouldn't do much good at this stage. The race will be under way in less than ten minutes."

Fargo did as others were doing and tied the ribbon around his left arm. "Happy now?"

"Very much so, thank you." The official took a step. "Is it me, sir, or are you a tad irritable today?"

"Mister, you don't know the half of it." Fargo looked down at the shoes, then at the ribbon, then at his saddlebags. "They have more to answer for than they think."

"Who does, sir?" the official cheerfully inquired.

"You'll read about it in the newspaper." On that cryptic note, Fargo moved toward the yellow stake that marked the start of the course. Someone he knew was already there.

"I would say good morning but I am afraid you would bite my head off." Swift Fox was a tribute to her name. "You glare at the world today."

"Not me. I'm a bundle of brotherly love." Fargo forced a smile for her benefit. Her feet, he saw, were naked, as they had been that first day. "Do you always run barefoot?"

"Since I was a child. I find I run faster. They are so thick with calluses, stones and sticks do not bother me." Swift Fox stared at his feet. "Your shoes are pretty."

Fargo made a solemn vow. Should he live to be a hundred, he would never wear anything but boots ever again.

"I must confess I am surprised you have entered the race."

"It wasn't my idea." Fargo was inclined to say more but Jonathan Quinby and Marshal Darnell had climbed onto a small platform and the lawman was motioning for quiet.

"Listen up, everyone! His honor, the mayor, would like to address you before we get things rolling!"

Quinby was all teeth and oily charm. "Ladies and gentlemen, welcome to the First Annual Nugget Chamber of Commerce Test of Endurance in the Art of Footracing. There were a few naysayers who claimed we couldn't pull it off, but look around. I want to personally thank each and every one of you for attending." Applause erupted, and Quinby lapped it up. "In a few moments our town marshal will discharge the starting gun, but first there are a few items we should cover."

Spike Yokum materialized beside Silvermane.

"Monitors have been posted at regular intervals. It is their job to ensure the race is conducted in a fair and orderly fashion." Quinby raked the crowd with a stern stare. "Nonparticipants are not allowed to have any contact with the runners. I can't stress this enough. Whoever violates this rule will be disqualified. No exceptions whatsoever."

Fargo swore the mayor was looking at him.

"To keep on top of things, dispatch riders have been assigned to various points along the course to provide updates to us here in town. Both they and the monitors wear tags identifying them as such."

Amarillo was moving toward the front. One look at him and other runners shied away.

"Water will be available every half mile thanks to the kind generosity of the Sisters of Charity. Contestants are urged to drink often to ward off the heat, but not too much at any one stop or you'll become waterlogged."

Fargo did a few knee bends, wishing they would get on with it. Marta must be beside herself with fear and worry; he couldn't wait to free her from Yokum's clutches. Then it would be his turn.

"The important thing is for everyone to have a good time," Quinby lied. "A lot of money is riding on the outcome, but it's not who wins or loses that's important. What counts most is the fine tradition of fair play and fun we're inaugurating here today."

It was a wonder he could say it with a straight face, Fargo mused.

"Our best guess is that the first runners will cross the finish line in two to three hours. Possibly more, given the heat and the difficulty. So you're all cordially invited to indulge in Nugget's hospitality until then." A rousing cheer went up. Quinby waited for it to subside, then nodded at the lawman. "Marshal Darnell, if you please. The moment we've all been waiting for has arrived."

A knot formed in Fargo's gut. He was letting himself in for one hell of a morning. Yet what choice did he have?

Drawing his revolver, the lawman pointed it into the air. "On the count of three!" he shouted. An air of excitement gripped the crowd and they surged forward to view the start. "One!"

Swift Fox dropped into a crouch, one hand on the ground.

"Two!"

Fargo tried to recollect the last time he had run more than a couple of miles at one stretch. It had to be ages ago. He dug in his heels.

"Three!" Darnell hollered, and half of those present roared along with him. His revolver cracked loud and clear.

Just like that, all the runners were in motion. Fargo found himself swept along in the thick of the pack. He lost sight of Swift Fox, who bolted like a doe being pursued by ravenous wolves. Amarillo was only a few steps behind her.

An elbow jostled Fargo on the left. A runner on the right nearly collided with him. Never one to like being hemmed in, Fargo put on a burst of speed. It wasn't wise to expend a lot of energy at the outset but he raced on ahead anyway. Once he was no longer surrounded, he slowed.

Breathing deep into his lungs, Fargo paced himself. The shoes felt strange but he would get used to them after a while. He rather liked how supple they were. They wouldn't chafe after hours of use.

The sun was merciless. Fargo hadn't gone twenty yards when he was caked in sweat. He imagined that by the time he reached the finish line he would be drenched. Up ahead was Luther Samuels, running smoothly. Swift Fox had outdistanced everyone and was well in the lead. As for Amarillo, the Apache did what Apaches were notorious for doing; he had disappeared and was nowhere to be seen.

After a hundred yards Fargo's legs grew abominably sore but the discomfort dropped to a tolerable level soon after. At three hundred yards he had a dull ache low down on his side. It persisted for the longest while. Thankfully, it never worsened to the point he had to stop.

The first monitor was at the five hundred yard mark, a mousey man in spectacles who grinned and waved as Fargo went by. "You're doing great, mister! There are only eleven runners in front of you."

"Is that all?" Fargo rounded a bend and spotted one, a young man favoring his left leg and limping every few steps. As he came even, the man glanced at him, then slowed.

"Damn! I think I sprained my ankle. Looks like I can kiss that ten thousand so long. Hope you do better."

"That makes two of us." Fargo slowed some, too.

In order to last the whole race he had to conserve as much strength as possible until the end. Driving his legs in measured cadence, he was hardly aware of the passage of time until he crossed over a rise and saw four runners in a cluster. Beyond, at the side of the trail, were a pair of women in brown dresses seated at a long table. Parked near them was a wagon fitted with a wooden water tank.

All four runners stopped to gulp water. By the time Fargo got there, they had resumed running. Halting, he leaned on the table, feeling drops of sweat trickle down his arms and chest.

"It sure is a scorcher, isn't it?" a Sister of Charity asked as she filled a glass from a pitcher.

"Land sakes, it tuckers me out just looking at you," joked her friend, pushing a tray toward him. "Would you care for a cracker and cheese? Or perhaps a handful of Saratoga chips?"

"This will do." Fargo downed the water in several swallows. As he set the glass down she reached over and placed her hand on his.

"Have you had your vegetables today? Eat your greens and you'll never want for stamina. That's what my grandmother always taught me, bless her sweet soul."

"Be sure to mention that to everyone else," Fargo suggested. Anything to slow the rest down, however slightly. He jogged westward, refreshed, but it didn't last long. The temperature was climbing rapidly. His body grew so hot, he felt he could burst into flame at any moment.

When all was said and done, the race truly was an endurance test, pitting men and women against the blistering desert and the stifling sun. As Richard Thorne had discovered, if one didn't get you, the other would. Fargo had crossed the desert so many times, he could endure it better than most. But was that enough to see him through to the end?

The four runners reappeared, one strung out after the other. They were locals. A couple of prospectors, a townsman in shirt sleeves and trousers, and a kid not much over sixteen. They were fairly fit and doing well enough so far but the heat was taking a toll.

Fargo soon overtook them and started to pass on the left. One of the prospectors was last, and the man deliberately veered to prevent him from going by. Fargo angled to the right but again the man blocked him, then glanced back, grinning.

"Your choice," Fargo said. Darting his right foot out, he hooked it between the prospector's legs. That was all it took to send the cheater tumbling. The man yelped and the others slowed, allowing Fargo to speed by before they knew what had happened.

"Hey!" the townsman bawled. "Come back here!"

"What did you do that for?" the second prospector hollered.

Fargo wasn't going to waste precious breath, and precious time, justifying what he had done. He ran a shade faster to increase his lead, then heard the patter of onrushing shoes. The others were after him, anger fueling their tired limbs.

"Hold up!" the townsman commanded. "We want to talk to you!"

Talk, hell, Fargo reflected, and ran faster. He had a ten yard lead but the townsman and the kid were whittling it down, their feet slapping the hard ground like hands striking a drum. Part of him wanted to turn and pound some sense into them but they were only doing what they thought was right. They hadn't seen the prospector cut him off. For the next hundred yards they pressed him but it proved to be their undoing. At last even the kid had to break off, breathing raggedly, his body pushed to the point of collapse.

The extra effort had cost Fargo, too. His buckskins were more soaked than ever, and so much sweat was trickling into his eyes, they stung like crazy. Brushing a sleeve across them, he saw another monitor, an elderly fellow who was sucking on a canteen. The sight caused his throat to go drier than it was.

"Hell of a hot day for a race," the monitor commented. "Next time maybe we should do this in the winter."

For Fargo there wouldn't be a next time. Running wasn't for him. He could never do it professionally, like Swift Fox and the earl. As a parson he once knew would say, if God had wanted man to run himself to death, He wouldn't have created horses.

No one was behind him now that Fargo could see. No one was in front of him when he reached the next water table. This time he sipped the glass slowly. Seldom had water tasted so delicious.

The Sisters of Charity watched with amusement. "My, you certainly are thirsty," one belabored the obvious.

"You have no idea, ma'am." Fargo's voice sounded strained. He craved another glass but too much might induce cramps. Removing his hat, he untied his bandanna, wet it, wrapped it around his forehead, and placed his hat back on over it. "How many are ahead of me, do you know?"

"I believe there are seven," one of the Sisters answered.

The other ticked them off on her fingers. "An Indian girl was in the lead. Then there was a black fellow, and that awful Apache with those horrible eyes. A couple of young fellows were after him. Oh, and Barney, the clerk at the bank. Plus one more who eludes me at the moment."

"Mr. Carpenter, dear," the other Sister said. "From the Comstock Mine. You remember. You commented on his big nose."

"My goodness. How could I forget? It's like a cucumber."

Their total tallied with what the first monitor had

told Fargo. "Thanks, ladies." He resumed running, feeling better than since he started. Maybe his body was adjusting. Maybe the years he had spent in the wilds, honing his body into solid muscle, were paying off in a way he had never foreseen.

At the four mile mark Fargo rounded a bend and nearly tripped over a man down on his hands and knees, retching. The stink was awful. If the size of the man's nose was any clue, it had to be, "Carpenter?"

The miner glanced up. "The heat! I can't take it any more!" He had a belly on him the size of a keg of ale and was clearly in no shape to run a ten-mile marathon. It was amazing he had made it this far. Clutching at Fargo's leg, he pleaded, "Please! Tell the next monitor I need a doctor!"

"I'll let him know," Fargo promised. It was several minutes before he spied the next one, though, on the crown of a low, barren hill. The man wasted no time climbing on his horse and trotting back to help.

The next leg of the course was essentially flat and straight. Fargo was running better than ever, the ache in his side long gone. Other than lingering stiffness in his calves, he was fine.

At the next stake Fargo passed a gasping, balding gnome in a store-bought outfit. It had to be Barney, the bank clerk, and he was staggering along as if drunk. He was also saying the same thing over and over again: "Think of the money! Think of the money! Think of the money!"

Fargo was surprised when he came to the halfway mark. He hadn't thought he had it in him. The Sisters of Charity helped a lot. Without their water, he wouldn't have made it this far.

For some time there had been no sign of Swift Fox, Amarillo or Luther Samuels, and Fargo rated his chances of catching up to them as slim. They had been over the course half a dozen times in practice runs. They knew it as he did the back of his hand. If he had laid down money on the outcome, he'd have bet on one of them.

Two runners loomed out of the haze. Country boys, wearing homespun britches and shoes with holes in them. Brothers, maybe, with the same wheat-hued hair, big ears, and more freckles than fawns had spots. They were breathing much too loudly, their legs pumping mechanically.

"Damn," one said as Fargo went by. "First the black passed us. Then the Injun. Now this feller. We might as well pack it in, Cletus. We ain't never gonna win this shebang."

"And here I reckoned we were a shoo-in."

The trail looped back toward Nugget. Boulders sprouted on either side, some as big as the Ovaro. Fargo crossed a series of gullies and came to a deep ravine. A yellow stake to the left showed which direction to go. Once on the other side he had to climb a steep slope made treacherous by loose dirt. At the top were more boulders, a virtual maze. More stakes, too, spaced close together, to guide the runners to an open space at the center. He had taken a few strides into it when he saw Swift Fox and Amarillo seated with their backs to a stone slab, their wrists bound. He tried to reverse direction but three rifles had swung toward him.

"Stop right there!" barked a fourth man, whose pencil frame was as bony as a skeleton. "This is as far as you go!"

10

Skye Fargo had been caught flat-footed. He consoled himself with the fact his senses had been dulled by fatigue. But that didn't lessen the sting of being pushed toward the stone slab, of being ordered to sit next to Swift Fox and Amarillo.

"Now hold out your arms," the skeleton directed, "so we can tie you good and proper. No funny stuff, you hear? You get to live so long as you don't give us any grief."

One other person was present, one Fargo didn't notice until an ebony figure stepped around from behind the riflemen.

"This ain't right. I don't need no help."

"Are you still here, Mr. Samuels?" the skeleton man said. "You should be on your way. We'll hold these three for five minutes or so, enough to guarantee they can't beat you into town."

"It's not right," Luther Samuels reiterated.

"Don't be a dunce. The mayor is looking out for your best interests, as well as his. You're the one who needs all that money to free your sweetheart. Think of her, and skedaddle."

"I said I'd run for him. We never talked about doing anything like this. If we had, I'd have told him no. I want to win, sure, but I want to do it fair and square."

"That's nice." The walking skeleton was becoming

annoyed. "Take it up with him after the race if you feel the need. But for now, get your black ass out of here."

"Don't talk to me like that."

The gunman sighed. "Didn't your mama ever tell you not to look a gift horse in the mouth? We're talking *ten thousand dollars*. Hell, that's more than some make in their lifetimes."

Samuels stubbornly stayed where he was. "I've never cheated at anything and I'm not startin' now. Let them go."

"I don't believe what I'm hearing." The skeleton glanced at his friends. "I don't know which is more stupid. Him making this much fuss when he's being handed ten grand on a silver platter, or him thinking he can boss white people around."

As hot tempered as ever, Samuels snarled and moved toward him, but at a nod from the skeleton, one of the riflemen slammed the butt of his weapon into the pit of Samuels's stomach, driving him to his knees. His floppy hat fell to the dirt.

"You're one dumb cuss, do you know that?" The skeleton stalked over, grabbed hold of Samuels's hair, and jerked his head up. "The only reason I don't split your skull is because Quinby wouldn't like it. But I swear, if you don't start using your head for something other than a hat rack, I'll look you up after the race and teach you to mind your betters."

Luther was doubled in agony. Glancing at Fargo, he grated through clenched teeth, "This was none of my doing. You've got to believe that."

"I believe you," Fargo said. The gunman about to tie his wrists, like those covering him, were looking at Samuels, not at him. The gunman's rifle was propped against the slab, inches from his arm. Suddenly whipping his right foot up into the man's groin, he snatched the rifle, a new Spencer, and was off the ground before they could think to stop him. He jammed the muzzle against the skeleton's cheek. "Guess who will die before I do if anyone else shoots?"

One of the riflemen took aim but a shriek from the skeleton stopped him. "Don't you dare! None of you!"

Indecision rooted them long enough for Luther Samuels to uncurl and wrench the rifle from the man who had struck him. The remaining gunman immediately pointed his weapon at the sky, saying, "Hell, we're not being paid enough to be turned into worm food."

Fargo stepped back and crouched to untie Swift Fox and Amarillo, but the wily Apache had slid a long-bladed knife from a knee-high moccasin, reversed his grip, and was deftly slicing the rope. Rising, Amarillo looked down at Swift Fox, and with a swift slash cut her rope, too, without breaking her skin.

"No hard feelings, right?" the skeleton said.

What happened next took everyone off guard, Fargo included. Amarillo took several quick steps, passing each of the gunmen on his way toward a yellow stake next to a gap that would take them out of the maze. In another heartbeat he was gone, his long hair flying.

Something moist and warm spattered Fargo's cheek. He heard Luther Samuels gasp, heard Swift Fox cry out in the Crow tongue. He touched his cheek and his palm came away slick with blood.

"God, no!" the skeletal gunman exclaimed. A scarlet spray was pumping from a severed artery in the side of his neck. Clasping his hands over the wound, he blurted in astonishment, "How did he do that? I didn't even see his hand move."

His companions couldn't answer. Each was oozing to the ground, their throats slit from ear to ear. One was already dead. Another was vainly trying to stem the flow. The third began flopping like a fish out of water and mewing like a dying cat.

"Help us!" the skeleton wailed. He tried to say more but blood spouted from his mouth and all that came out was a gurgling mumble. Pitching to his hands and knees, he looked around in dismay, and died.

Samuels covered his mouth and turned, gagging.

Swift Fox stepped back so none of the spray stained her doeskin dress and remarked, "Evidently, Apaches do not care about offending whites as much as Crows do."

Fargo didn't feel the least bit sorry for them. There was an old saying, taken from one even older; those who lived by the gun, died by the gun. He dropped the Spencer. "I won't say a word if you don't."

Swift Fox moved past him, grinning. "We can discuss it at the finish line if you do not take too long getting there."

About to follow, Fargo had to abruptly dig in his heels to avoid colliding with Luther Samuels, whose queasiness had given way to panic.

"That Apache got the jump on us! But I ain't lettin' him win my ten thousand dollars! No sir! He'll get it over my dead body!"

Fargo was last out of the boulders. He didn't push himself. It would be pointless. The other three were faster than he was. He would gladly settle for coming in fourth. All that mattered to Spike Yokum was that Samuels didn't win. Anyone else was fine. And with the lead the two Indians had, Fargo was confident Samuels didn't have a snowball's chance in Hades of winning. He could relax a bit, take his time.

The miles drifted by. Fargo passed the six mile stake. The seven. The eight. His legs were cramping but not severely enough to bring him to stop. He negotiated a steep grade. On the crown was another water table, and two Sisters of Charity staring warily at a swarthy figure seated on the ground on the far side of the trail.

Amarillo had removed his left moccasin and was

examining his ankle. A protrusion above it told the story; he had broken it.

Stupefied, Fargo drew up short. "How did that happen?"

The Apache didn't answer.

Dashing to the table, Fargo asked, "Can you tell me how far ahead the others are?"

"A minute or two at the most." One of the Sisters nodded at the Mimbre. "He slipped coming up the grade, yonder."

"That's right," verified the other. "He wasn't paying attention. Looking over his shoulder when he should have been watching his step. A rock slid out from under him and down he tumbled."

An oath was on the tip of Fargo's tongue but he didn't give voice to it. Apaches were as surefooted as mountain goats. To have something like this happen was a one in a million fluke. But he had no reason to worry. Swift Fox was still ahead of Samuels. She should win, easily.

Then the first Sister of Charity made a comment that filled him with dread. "It's a shame about the Indian girl. Her hurting herself, and all."

"What?"

"She was favoring her right leg when she came by," said the second Sister. "Must have pulled a muscle or something."

The first Sister made a tsk-tsk sound. "You should have heard the black man laugh when he went by. Rubbing her misfortune in her nose like that. How awful." She held a glass aloft. "Care for some water?"

"No time," Fargo said, and poured on the speed. He ran flat out, not caring if his legs protested, not caring if his muscles wouldn't stop cramping. He couldn't let Samuels win. Marta's life was at stake. At the top of every rise he scoured the next stretch of trail for Swift Fox and Samuels but didn't spot them. He wasn't keeping track of the distance he covered, so when another yellow stake reared out of the earth, shock spiked through him. Painted on it in large black letters were the words, MILE NUMBER NINE.

Only one mile to go! Fargo's lungs were straining and his feet hurt terribly, but all he could think of was Marta. For her sake he endured the pain. For her sake he pressed on, pushing himself to his limit and beyond. He couldn't shake a mental image of Silvermane putting a Smith and Wesson to her temple and squeezing the trigger.

Presently buildings framed the horizon. Band music rose to the cloudless sky, underscored by a dull roar. The good citizens of Nugget were cheering on the lead runner.

A heaviness seeped into Fargo's limbs, a sensation that had nothing to do with his state of near exhaustion and everything to do with the fact that he had failed. He couldn't possibly overtake Samuels. Yokum would be furious. No excuse would be good enough, no explanation would stop him from venting his wrath on Marta.

The cheers grew louder. Judging by the frenzy, the race was almost won. It was useless but Fargo tried to run faster. He didn't have it in him. His body had used all its reserves, and then some. Willpower was all that kept his legs moving.

Fargo came around the last bend and saw spectators mobbing the winner. They were whooping and hollering like there was no tomorrow. Hardly anyone noticed him cross the finish line. By then he was plodding along on leaden legs, his lungs were close to collapse. Stopping, he placed his hands on his hips and bent over. His stomach was churning. He might be sick.

"I can't believe she beat me."

In the shadow of the special stand for the dignitaries sagged Luther Samuels. His shoulders slumped, he was the portrait of defeat.

Fargo couldn't credit his own eyes. Sucking in air, he gasped in disbelief, "Swift Fox won?"

Samuels raised his fists to the sides of his head, closed his eyes, and groaned. "She came out of nowhere. One second I was all by myself, on top of the world, and the next she was right on my heels." He leaned his forehead against a post. "Once the town came in sight, she took off like a bat out of hell and left me eating her dust. I never saw anything like it."

Fargo was so elated, he yipped for joy.

"I'm glad someone is happy," Samuels said bitterly. "I sure as hell ain't. Now I don't have the money to buy my gal's freedom."

"There are other races."

Samuels straightened. "That there are! Sante Fe is hostin' one soon. The prize is three thousand. Well worth my while. After that, Denver. Then Kansas City." He smiled. "Maybe we'll compete again some day."

"The day I do this again," Fargo declared, "is the day buffalo sprout wings and fly."

Chuckling, Samuels shuffled toward the crowd. "Reckon I'd better see the mayor about the second place prize money. Not that he'd try anything with all these people around, but I don't trust him any further than I can throw one of those flyin' buffalo of yours."

Fargo had business of his own to attend to. Stumbling to the stand, he sat on the steps to collect his breath. Thanks to the uproar and his own loud breathing, he didn't realize someone had come over until he looked up.

"If I'd wanted to kill you just now, it would have been easy as sin," Silvermane remarked.

"Is there something you want?" Fargo made no attempt to hide his dislike. He knew, as surely as he was sitting there, that before he left Nugget the two of them would swap lead.

"Mr. Yokum is pleased you held up your end. Now he'll hold up his. He'll have the girl at his saloon in two hours."

"No. In ten minutes."

The gunfighter sneered. "You're in no position to make demands. The boss has to be on hand here when the prize money is handed out, him being a bigwig and all. It'll be a while before he can get away."

Fargo would have loved to wipe that sneer off Silvermane's face with his fist, but he had to sit there, spent, as the man in black sauntered away. A figure hobbling on crutches gave the gunfighter a wide berth.

"Mr. Fargo! Blimey, you put on a bloody good show. Third place, unless I'm mistaken." Desmond Sherwood was all smiles. "Ever think of becoming a professional runner?" At his side was Penelope Ashton, her hair shimmering like golden straw in the sunlight.

"Only if I go insane." Fargo's chest wasn't hurting as bad but his legs felt like they weighed tons. "Didn't expect to see you up and around so soon."

"What? Miss the race? Are you daft?" Sherwood winked at Penelope. "That will be the day, right luv?"

Penelope hadn't taken her eyes off Fargo. "May I add my compliment to his? Your stamina, sir, is most impressive. I daresay you could go all day and all night if you had to."

"Not now I couldn't," Fargo responded. "Look me up after I've had a day or two of rest."

The earl braced himself on his crutches. "Damnable invention, these. But they keep me from falling flat on my face so I shouldn't complain." He scanned the madhouse the street had become. "I'm surprised your lady friend, Miss Endelstrom, isn't here to congratulate you."

"We saw her on our way here," Penelope mentioned. "I waved but she didn't wave back. The rude wench."

Fargo forgot his fatigue and rose. "Where was this?"

"She was at a second-floor window on Fremont Street," Penelope informed him. "Just sort of staring off into space and looking as glum as could be."

Gripping her arms, Fargo asked, "Which window? I need to know exactly." Two hours was too long to wait. There was no telling what might happen to Marta.

Wincing, Penelope pulled back. "I didn't notice the address. It was above the butcher shop, directly across from the Sagebrush Corral."

Fargo forced his balking legs to move. He had to get there before the festivities concluded. After wasting fifteen minutes hiking to the Ovaro, and strapping on his Colt, he wearily stepped into the stirrups.

Most of the streets were deserted. Fremont ran from north to south on Nugget's east side, and was largely lined by businesses. He reined up around the corner from the corral, tied the Ovaro to a rail, and moved under an overhang to study the street without being seen. A large sign pinpointed the butcher's. Above the shop were two windows, curtains drawn.

Pulling his hat low and slouching, Fargo reached the corner. A CLOSED sign hung on the door. At the back, a flight of stairs gave access to the second floor. He drew the Colt and tiptoed up. Placing his ear to the door, he heard voices.

"—down and quit your complaining. I'm sick and tired of hearing your prattle." Mitch wasn't in a good mood. "I wish to hell Yokum would send word so we can get this over with."

"You and me, both," said another man. "I don't like being cooped up."

A third hired gun chimed in with, "What I don't like is missing the race. I have forty dollars riding on that Apache, and I'd like to know how it turned out."

Fargo gingerly tried the latch. It rose quietly but the door wouldn't budge, even when he put his shoulder to it. Mitch was saying something but he couldn't make out what it was. He knocked twice, loudly, then put his free hand over his mouth to disguise his voice and growled, "Open up! I have a message from Yokum!"

The gambit worked. Someone threw the bolt and the door swung in. A startled gunman belted out a warning a split-second before Fargo caught him flush on the forehead with the Colt's barrel. A single step and Fargo was inside. Mitch lounged on a settee against the left wall. Over by the window was the other gunman, sprawled in an easy chair. Fargo covered them. "Where is she?"

"You!" Anger nearly brought Mitch to his feet. "How the hell did you find us?"

Fargo took deliberate aim at a spot a hand's length below Mitch's gun belt. "I won't ask a second time."

"She's in the bedroom!" Mitch pointed to a closed door across the room. "We haven't laid a finger on her. Honest! So don't be hasty with that hog leg."

Fargo called Marta's name. The bedroom door opened and she poked her head out. Beaming, she rushed toward him, so happy to see him, she didn't realize the mistake she was making. Fargo did, though, and opened his mouth to tell her to stop. But the command had barely formed in his throat when she blundered in front of the gunman in the easy chair.

Fargo immediately stepped to the left and it was well he did. The gunman had gone for his six-shooter. "Don't!" Fargo warned, without effect. As the man's revolver rose, he squeezed off two swift shots. The first blast kicked the gunman back, the second knocked him across the arm of the chair.

Expecting a slug in the side, Fargo pivoted. But Mitch hadn't resorted to his Remington. He was bolting for the front door.

Fargo had a clear shot at Mitch's back, but he gave chase instead. Mitch slammed the door in his face and he yanked on the latch. "Hold it!"

Mitch was halfway down, taking the stairs four at a jump. Twisting in midjump, he jerked his revolver.

The jamb exploded into slivers inches from Fargo's eyes, and he banged off two shots of his own. Mitch somersaulted heels over head down the remaining steps and crashed to earth like a fallen sapling, with an audible *crack*. He tried to lift his head, screamed "Nooooo!" and went limp.

A hand fell on Fargo's shoulders. He turned, and Marta melted into his arms in gratitude. "You're safe now."

Marta was trembling. She clung to him, her nails digging into his shoulders, tears dampening her cheeks. "They were fixing to use me to get to you. I overheard them. Something about setting a trap later."

So much for Spike Yokum being a man of his word. Fargo ushered her down the stairs. With all the racket the celebrants were raising, it was unlikely the marshal had heard the shots. But it was better to make themselves scarce anyway.

Marta couldn't stop trembling. Or talking. "I've never been so scared in my life. Yokum paid another girl to tell me you wanted to see me out back of the saloon where I work, and like a fool I fell for it. Mitch and those other two brought me here in a buckboard. I gave them a piece of my mind, but Mitch took to slapping me every time I opened my mouth so I stopped."

They reached the last step. Fargo listened but heard nothing to indicate anyone was coming to investigate. Holding Marta close, he hurried west along the rear of the buildings.

"What are we going to do? Where can we go? Not my apartment, that's for sure."

"Anywhere else you can lay low until I do what needs to be done?"

Marta arched an eyebrow. "Please don't. Not on my behalf. Can't you ride out and let them be?"

"Not if I aim to look at myself in the mirror ever again, no." Fargo peeked past the corner. The side street was empty. "There are things a man has to do if he wants to go on calling himself a man."

"Please be careful." Marta traced his jaw with a finger. "I never did get my second helping."

Fargo jogged toward the Ovaro. They had to cross Fremont Street but he reasoned it should be safe enough. Then he heard Marta's sharp intake of breath.

Coming toward them were four gunmen on horseback. One was a lot smaller than the rest, and favored black clothes and a black hat.

"Damn." Fargo pushed Marta ahead of him. They were right out in the open, so it was no wonder a fuzz-faced lobo with better vocal chords than brains yipped in recognition and went for his six-gun. Fargo fired first, and scored. He snapped off a second shot but the others had spurred their horses and he missed.

"Get them!" Spraying lead, two of the riders bore down.

Fargo thumbed back the hammer and stroked the trigger a third time, but a *click* reminded him he had neglected to replace the spent cartridges after shooting Mitch. The Ovaro was only half a block away but it might as well be in California. The gunmen would be on top of them before they reached it.

Without breaking stride, Fargo ducked into the recessed doorway of a dry goods store. Fingers flying, he emptied the Colt and began reloading. He had only two new cartridges in the cylinder when hooves thundered and the two gunmen trotted by. A few yards shy of the Ovaro the pair drew rein and twisted in their saddles, searching all over.

Fargo slid a third and a fourth cartridge into the Colt.

"Where the hell did they get to?"

Fargo had the last two cartridges in his left hand. All he needed was another couple of seconds.

"There they are!" Both gunmen wheeled their mounts. Lead and smoke spewed from their shooting irons.

Holes pockmarked the windows on either side as Fargo took aim. His Colt boomed. One of the guns-for-hire screamed and keeled from the saddle. He aimed at the other killer as the door behind him thudded to an impact. Again the Colt boomed, and the gunman joined his partner on the ground. His nerves as taut as piano wire, Fargo crept to the end of the boardwalk.

Silvermane sat on his horse smack in the middle of Fremont, his hands on his saddle horn. "Nicely done. I knew they didn't stand a prayer." The man in black raised his reins. "I'll be with Yokum. Don't keep me waiting too long or you'll die slow and hard."

Tendrils of dust hung in the air for a full minute after he was gone.

11

The Tumbleweed Hotel was located on the north side of town, farther from the celebration than any other, which was part of the reason Skye Fargo picked it. The other factor was that, as far as Marta knew, it wasn't owned by Spike Yokum or the mayor.

The lobby, like the street, was empty save for a frumpy desk clerk roused from a newspaper he was reading. "If you're looking for a room, you can forget it. We're booked up, just like every other place in town."

Marta leaned over the counter, highlighting her cleavage. "You don't sound very happy about it."

"Why should I be? I just work here." The man was a born grump. "Here I am, stuck behind this stupid desk while everyone else is having the time of their lives. Is that fair, I ask you?" He answered his own question. "No, it's not."

Marta tapped the register. "Are you sure you can't find a room for little old me? I don't take up a lot of space."

"Just you?" The clerk glanced uncertainly at Fargo.

Marta smiled her most innocent smile. "Him? He's my brother. In town for the race, but he's leaving tomorrow. I'm letting him stay at my apartment since he's flat broke. Since I'm partial to my privacy, I figured to take a room for the night." She batted her eyelashes. "Even a closet would do."

The clerk tugged at his collar, then cleared his throat. "There is one vacant at the moment. It's been reserved for a couple from Salt Lake City but they were due yesterday and never arrived. I suppose I could let you have it. But if they show up I could get into hot water."

Giggling, Marta touched his cheek. "I wouldn't want to get a good-looking gentleman like you into any trouble. But I would be ever so grateful."

"Good-looking?" The clerk's complexion was the same as a beet's. "Tell you what. I'll let you have the room. If they show up, I'll return their deposit and advise them to find lodgings elsewhere. So long as they don't complain to Mr. Pennyworth, there shouldn't be any problem."

"You're a dear, do you know that?" Marta grinned in delight and pinched his knobby chin.

The clerk insisted on escorting them upstairs. He stumbled twice because he couldn't tear his eyes off Marta's bosom, and when they reached the room, bleated, "Anything you want, ma'am, anything at all, you say the word and it's yours."

"Aren't you a darling?" Accepting the key, Marta bestowed a seductive look hot enough to melt a candle. "I may just take you up on that." When he continued to stand there, mesmerized by her beauty, she took him by the shoulders, slowly turned him around, and swatted him on the backside. "Run along for now. We'll talk more later." Crestfallen, he shambled off.

"Men!" Marta said under her breath. "They're easier to lead around than dogs on a leash."

"Oh?" Fargo stepped up behind her and cupped her bottom.

"Most of them," Marta smiled. Quickly opening the door, she snagged his wrist and hauled him in after her. "Now I can thank you properly for saving my life." She threw the bolt and pressed herself against him, her hips grinding into his.

132

"Don't get yourself excited. I have something to do."

"Can't it wait?" Marta nuzzled his throat. "I need to catch some sleep but my nerves have been rubbed raw." She licked his ear. "You could help me relax enough to sleep like a baby."

Fargo couldn't deny she was having an effect. Maybe it wouldn't hurt to let her have her way. Yokum was bound to be furious once he learned she had escaped; it would serve him right to stew a while. He ran his hand down one thigh.

"Do I take that as a 'yes'?"

Fargo's reply was to cover her soft mouth with his. He was still fatigued from the race, but the twitching in his groin proved he wasn't too tired to rise to the occasion. She helped matters by lowering a hand to his manhood and rubbing it through his pants.

"Mmmm," Marta murmured. "Is this a tree limb or are you happy I asked you to stick around?" She skipped to the bed and stripped off her clothes in a third of the time it would have taken him. Then she lay on her back and patted the quilt. "Are you waiting for an engraved invite?"

Fargo shed his gun belt and shirt and sat on the edge to remove his boots. She never gave him the chance. Grabbing his shoulders, she pulled him down flat onto his back. "In a rush, are you?"

"Handsome, you don't know what it was like," Marta said between tiny nibbles on his neck and ear. "I wanted you the other night, wanted you so much. Then those jackasses came along and spoiled everything." She rimmed his navel with her moist tongue. "I couldn't stop thinking about you the whole time, about what I had missed, about what I might never get to do again."

Fargo smiled as she unhitched his pants and tugged them down below his hips. His breath caught in his throat when his member was enveloped in an exquisite wetness.

Marta raised her head, her eyes twinkling. "Like that, do you? Good thing for you I do, too." Her head dropped again.

The seconds blurred into one another, the minutes into an unending stream of pleasure. Fargo let her have her way with him, let her stoke him to a feverish pith, let her kiss every square inch of skin from his ankles to his forehead and back down again. When she straddled him, he held himself still to make it easier for her to guide his pole where she wanted it to go.

"Ahhhhh. Yessssssssss."

Her throaty purr kindled Fargo's own desire. Grasping her hips, he bucked up into her.

"Oh!" Marta threw her head back, her lips parted wide. For several seconds she was transformed into a living sculpture of pure passion. At his next thrust, she bent low to fasten her mouth to his and greedily sucked on his tongue.

Fargo felt her breasts on his chest, felt hard nipples nudge his skin. He pinched one and her inner walls contracted on his pole, heightening the thrill. He pinched the other and she moaned loud enough to be heard down in the lobby.

"The things you do to me," Marta panted.

It wasn't one-sided, by any stretch. Fargo inhaled a breast and bit the nipple lightly with his front teeth. Again her tunnel squeezed him, a pattern he repeated over and over by switching from one breast to the other and back again.

Her back arched, Marta rode him like a rodeo rider on a bronco. She met his thrusts with downward plunges of her thighs, her feet splayed across his legs, her toenails scraping his calves. Placing her hands flat on his chest, she gained extra leverage and pumped ever faster, ever harder.

Under them the bed rattled and bounced. It was barely big enough for one person, let alone two, but the frame was sturdy, and that was all that counted. Like a piston in a steam engine, he speared up at her with more vigor than he thought he had left.

"Ahhhh," Marta exhaled. "I'm so wet, so very wet!"

Fargo wouldn't argue there. He was soaked from his hips down, drenched in the sweet nectar flowing from her fount. A tightening in his throat warned him that his explosion was near but he refused to gush before she did. Shutting his mind to the pleasure, he sought to sweep her over the crest by lathering her ear, her neck, her mounds. But it wasn't until he pinched both nipples that she soared to new heights, and hovered.

"More! More!" Marta puffed, her hair hiding half her face. "I'm so close, handsome. So close."

Fargo raked her back with his nails, and dug them into the swell of her buttocks. She shook like someone in the throes of a fit, only hers was a fit of utter abandon. Between her groans and the pounding of the bed, Fargo almost missed the light series of knocks on their door.

"Miss Endelstrom?"

It was the damn desk clerk. Fargo figured someone had complained, then remembered everyone was off celebrating.

"Miss Endelstrom? Please. This is important."

"Not now!" Fargo growled. He suspected the clerk might have been out in the hall the whole time, listening, and imagined the clerk was upset that Marta had lied to him. *To hell with it*, he decided, and thrust harder.

Marta was lost in bliss. "Skye!" she abruptly cried. Her thighs clamped tight and she spurted. "Oh God! Oh God! Oh God!"

Fargo preferred to last a while longer but his body

refused. The pent-up dam burst. He gushed until he was drained dry, then slowly coasted to a stop. Content to lie there savoring the aftermath, he was less than pleased when another light rap intruded itself.

"Please! I really must speak to one of you. It's urgent!"

"What on earth?" Marta blurted, sliding off Fargo. "Is that who I think it is? How long has he been out there?"

"I'll handle this." Fargo slid off the bed and buckled his pants. "This had better be important," he said as he opened the door.

The clerk was wringing his hands and wriggling like a worm on a hook. "I'm terribly sorry to disturb you. Honest I am. But something just happened and I thought you should know."

Fargo waited.

"Several men were here. Tough characters. They said they were searching for a man and woman answering your descriptions. That it would be worth fifty dollars if I informed them if you showed up."

"What did you say?"

"Why, that I never set eyes on either of you, of course." The clerk shifted to peer into the bedroom and his eyes nearly bugged out of his head. "They wouldn't tell me why they were after you."

Fargo pulled the door partway shut. "You did the right thing. If they show up again let me know."

"Sure thing, Mr. Fargo." Smiling and bobbing his head like a buzzard eating carrion, he backed away. "You can count on me."

Fargo had closed and bolted the door and taken several steps when it hit him that the clerk had called him by name. "We never told him who I was."

Marta was on her back, dreamily toying with her hair. "Maybe those men he mentioned did. Maybe he recognized you. Hell, you've been the talk of the town since you got here."

"If he recognized me, why didn't he call me by my name earlier?" Fargo retrieved his other clothes.

"What do you think you're doing?" Marta patted the blanket. "Get your redwood over here. We're not done yet."

"I'll only be a minute." Fargo was probably making a mountain out of a fly speck but he couldn't shake an urge to have a talk with the clerk. He strapped on his gun belt and jammed his hat on his head. "If I take too long, start without me."

Marta stuck her tongue out at him. "I might just do that to spite you. It would serve you right."

The hotel was unnaturally still. Treading softly so as not to scrape his soles on the polished hardwood floor, Fargo crept to the landing. The only sound from below was the lobby clock striking half past the hour. Feeling slightly foolish, he descended. He had only ten or twelve steps to go when someone coughed.

"What if he doesn't come down? What if he stays up there for the rest of the day?" The question was posed by the clerk.

"We're in no rush. Our orders are to have him pushing up weeds. There's no deadline."

Fargo had never heard the second voice before. He peered over the railing. The desk clerk was scribbling on a sheet of paper. Otherwise, the lobby appeared deserted.

He heard gruff cursing from the other side. "I don't like this damn waitin' around. I say we march up there and get this over with."

"Keep that trap of yours shut, Hemsley," came a reply from behind the front desk. "There's no telling when they might take it into their heads to come down."

Another gunman was hidden in a closet directly under the stairs. "I don't give a damn when or how we do it. Just so it gets done. I owe him for killing my brother yesterday."

So there were three, all told. Fargo drew his Colt. He would like to learn who sent them, although what real difference did it make? Yokum and Quinby were cut from the same cruel cloth. They were cold-hearted coyotes who didn't have the grit to do their own killing and hired it out to assassins like these.

The clerk glanced down at whoever was crouched next to him. "I don't see why I have to stay, Mr. Barnes. I'm putting myself in harm's way for a paltry hundred dollars."

"You didn't think it was so paltry when I offered it to you," was Barnes's retort. "We need you here so Fargo won't suspect anything is wrong. Savvy?"

"I still don't like it. If I take a bullet in a vital organ, I'll never get to spend your blood money."

The crown of a hat appeared. "It's not like we twisted your arm to help, is it? So stand there and shut up. If you ruin this for us, being shot will be the least of your worries."

"I'm not doing this for the money," the clerk insisted. "I have a civic duty to the town to cooperate as fully as I can."

"Good thing I'm wearing boots," Barnes declared, and the other two gunmen laughed.

Fargo launched himself over the rail. There would never be a better time; they were jabbering like chipmunks instead of concentrating on the job. Landing next to the closet door, which hung open several inches, he saw a vague shape move. He fired once and dived behind a rocking chair.

The clerk shrieked in terror.

Barnes rose to shoot, exposing himself. So did Hemsley by the sofa. Fargo banged off two swift shots and hit Hemsley high in the shoulder. Both ducked back down.

Out of the closet staggered the third man. He was gut shot. Blood-caked fingers pressed over the wound, he turned toward Fargo, his revolver rising. "Kill you!" he screeched. "Kill you for my brother and me!"

Rolling onto his side, Fargo cored the gunman's brain. Shots peppered the floor and the wall as he scrambled toward the near end of the front desk.

The fear-struck clerk picked that moment to bolt toward the street. In doing so, he blundered between Fargo and the gunmen. His last earthly experience was that of having a slug enter his right temple and exit out the other, taking a sizeable chunk of his head along with it.

"Damn it, Hemsley, you idiot!" Barnes fumed. "We're not supposed to kill anyone else!"

The front desk was constructed of pine. It was sturdy enough for its purpose, but the front and side panels weren't more than a quarter-inch thick. Fargo fired at where he figured Barnes was crouched and there was a dull thud.

"Barnes?" Hemsley shouted. "Did he get you?"

The bottom of the sofa was several inches above the floor. Placing his cheek flat, Fargo glimpsed a pair of boots between the sofa and the wall. Extending both arms, he adopted a two-handed grip. An ankle filled his vision, and he squeezed the trigger.

The blast added more acrid gunsmoke to the swirling cloud rising toward the ceiling. A scream punctuated it. The gunman named Hemsley did what most anyone would do under similar circumstances; he lurched erect, clinging to the sofa, his face screwed up in torment.

"You shot me, you son of a bitch!"

"Why so surprised?" Fargo responded, and shot him again. Through the sternum this time, as Hemsley was leveling a pistol.

Fargo darted to the front desk. He had heard Barnes fall but it was no guarantee the man was dead. He looked over the top.

The gunman had fallen onto his side. His chest was

slowly rising and falling, and red spittle flecked his mouth. Well out of his reach lay a six-shooter.

Fargo walked to the rear of the counter. "You're not long for this world. Might as well tell me. Was it Mayor Quinby who hired you?"

Barnes tried to talk but suffered a coughing fit that spewed a crimson torrent from his nose and ears. "It was him."

"Where is he now?" Fargo wasn't particular about the order in which he settled his scores. The mayor might as well be first.

"No idea." Barnes coughed some more. "I told him it would take more than three of us but he wouldn't listen. Always thinks he knows it all."

"You made your bed, you pay the price." Fargo turned to go.

"Wait." Barnes struggled to raise his head but couldn't. "He's got a meeting with Yokum. Six this evening. There's a truce until then."

"Where?"

"Neutral ground. The Havlock Saloon at Fourth and Standish." Barnes's neck and shirt were stained crimson. "Shoot him once for me, will you?" Gritting his teeth, he flailed at the air with one hand, then went limp.

Fargo turned to go upstairs. The movement saved his life. At the front of the lobby a revolver boomed, and the slug intended for his head bored into the wall instead. Whirling, he glimpsed someone backpedaling out: Marshal Tom Darnell had just tried to murder him.

Racing to the door, Fargo paused. He pushed on it and another slug missed his hat by a hair. Tucking at the waist, he threw himself onto the boardwalk. Darnell was two buildings down, dodging around a corner. Fargo raised the Colt but not fast enough.

The lawman didn't reappear. Fargo waited a suitable interval, then rose and ran as fast as his strained sinews allowed to the mouth of the alley Darnell had entered. It connected to a side street, which Fargo scrutinized from end to end.

The lawman had made himself scarce.

By and large Fargo respected any man brave enough to pin on a badge. Most were decent, hard-working souls who did their best to apply the law fairly and reasonably. But every barrel had a few bad apples, and Tom Darnell was rotten to the core. Darnell had crossed the line no lawman could cross and still claim to be a guardian of the peace.

Marta was still in bed when Fargo returned. By rights he should join her. He was sore and stiff and tired as hell, but sleep had to wait. So too, amazingly enough, could another helping of her charms. "Get some rest. I'll be back in a few hours to take up where we left off."

"You're leaving me alone?" Marta had slid under the sheets but they only came to her waist. Her breasts were ripe melons just waiting to be fondled. "What about Yokum?"

"By tonight he won't ever kidnap anyone again." Fargo remembered to reload this time.

"I heard the shooting. I was scared sick something had happened to you. I like you, handsome. Like you a lot. If you ever get a hankering to dig in roots, look me up."

Fargo avoided the subject by saying, "How did a polecat like Quinby ever get elected? Don't the people here see for him what he is?"

"Of course." Marta sat up and the sheet slid lower. "It's no different in Nugget than anywhere else. Most don't care much about politics. They vote for whoever promises them the moon."

Fargo had to force himself to concentrate on the Colt and not her body.

"Quinby promised to turn Nugget into a city. The merchants backed him to line their pockets. The newspaper pushed for him so they'd have more readers. As for the people, well, let's just say that buying drinks every night at every saloon in town didn't hurt his chances any."

Fargo had seen the same pattern repeated elsewhere. It wasn't always the best candidate who won. "How many years left in his term?"

"About three." Marta eyed him quizzically. "Why this sudden interest in the town's political future?"

"Just curious, is all." Fargo was ready. Scrupulously avoiding her magnificent globes, he bent and kissed her. "Don't open the door for anyone." He gave her a revolver he had taken from one of the dead gunmen. "If you have to, use this."

"I hope you know what you're doing, lover. With the mayor and Yokum both out to bury you, you'll have to watch your back every second." Marta stroked his cheek. "Make it back alive and I'll give you a night you'll never forget."

Fargo had one last word of advice as he went out the door. "Bolt this behind me. And whatever you do, keep away from the window."

Marta grinned half-heartedly. "You're worse than a mother hen."

A few flies were buzzing around the blood on the lobby floor. Fargo left the bodies where they had fallen, and mounted up. He rode east, then south, using side streets and alleys. The only signs of life were an old man rooting through a stack of old crates and a gray cat preening itself on a porch.

The Quinby Hotel was like the man it was named after; showy but cheap. A dozing clerk jumped when Fargo pounded on the front desk. "Does the mayor have a room here?"

Smoothing his shirt, the kid tried to look important. "Room nothing. He has a whole suite. He owns this place, you know."

"Take me up."

"What? I can't do that unless he's given his permission."

Fargo drew his Colt and gouged the barrel against the bridge of the clerk's nose. "Take me up."

The suite was furnished with the best money could buy. Furniture, crystal lamps, fine china, jade figurines, paintings and much more. The cost had to be in the tens of thousands, far more than a humble civil servant could afford.

"Open the window," Fargo directed.

Perplexed, the kid did as he had been told. "Now what, mister?"

"Start throwing everything out into the street."

The kid laughed, thinking it was some kind of warped joke, but he quickly sobered. "I wouldn't want to be in your boots when Mayor Quinby finds out. He'll be mad enough to burst a blood vessel."

Fargo grinned. "That's the general idea."

12

The Havlock Saloon was booming. Men were lined up four deep at the bar. Games of chance, from poker and faro to dice, engrossed players at every table but one, which was reserved for a special meeting due to take place any minute. An unopened bottle of the finest whiskey had been set out, along with two glasses polished to a sheen.

In a nook to one side and slightly to the rear of the bar, Skye Fargo watched the bat-wing doors. He wasn't worried about being spotted. Not with sixty or seventy customers crammed in there like so many stalks of corn in a field. He was invisible in the shadows, nursing some red-eye.

The doors opened promptly at six. Silvermane strutted in first. All the gunfighter had to do was glare and a path was cleared for him and his employer.

Spike Yokum did not look happy. An unlit cigar jutted from his mouth, and he was chewing on it in a fury. He showed no more interest in the revelers than he would in a bunch of ants. Taking a seat so he faced the street, he opened the whiskey bottle and poured himself a stiff one. His pint-sized bodyguard assumed a post at his right elbow.

Always the crafty politician, Mayor Jonathan Quinby arrived last. At his side was Marshal Darnell. Pumping the hand of every man he passed, Quinby put on quite a show. Someone shoved a mug of beer at him and he accepted it with a flourish. He drained it before he reached the corner table. "I'm glad you didn't change your mind, Spike."

Yokum sniffed as if he had caught wind of manure. "This had better be important. I've got better things to do with my time than listen to you praise yourself to death."

"Such as replacing the liquor you lost at your saloon?" Quinby snapped his fingers at Darnell and the lawman dutifully pulled out a chair.

Yokum's foul mood worsened. "So you heard, did you? The gall of that bastard! Fargo marched in, held everyone at gunpoint, and made the bartender shatter every damn bottle. Two thousand dollars' worth!"

"Consider yourself fortunate. Mr. Fargo paid my hotel room a visit and destroyed ten times that amount in personal property." Quinby snapped his fingers again and Darnell filled his glass. "He's part of the reason I asked to meet with you. We must put a stop to his shenanigans."

"Work together?" Yokum snorted. "That would take some getting used to."

"Why? Because we've constantly been at odds?" The mayor removed his bowler. "I've been giving our bickering a lot of thought and I've come to the conclusion we've both been as dumb as adobe bricks. Rather than each doing his best to destroy the other, we should pool our resources and take over Nugget lock, stock and barrel."

Yokum smirked. "I swear. You would try to talk the rattles off a rattlesnake. But I'm not falling for it."

"Hear me out. That's all I ask." Quinby idly gazed toward the bar and for a moment Fargo thought the mayor saw him. But no, Quinby leaned forward to make his pitch. "For months the two of us have been tearing at one another like rabid dogs. We each want to be the leader of the pack, but all we ever really do is squander time and money we could put to a wiser use."

"You're babbling in circles like always."

"Am I? Think what we could achieve if we pooled our resources. Between the two of us we control seventy percent of Nugget. Together, we could raise that to one hundred percent. Instead of one leader of the pack, there would be two."

"Until my back is turned and you bury a knife in it. Nice try."

The mayor was either a first-rate actor or his regret was genuine. "I've never been more sincere in my life. I honestly don't see any reason why we can't share the seats of power. Me, on the political front. You, behind the scenes. Within a year we would be richer than either of us ever dreamed."

Fargo sidled to the right, keeping a knot of miners in front of him so he wouldn't be detected. It was time to end this.

"You expect me to trust *you*?" Yokum and Silvermane laughed, and Yokum added, "Why don't I stick my head in a bear's mouth while I'm at it?"

The insult wasn't appreciated. "I resent your attitude. Frankly, I credited you with more intelligence." Quinby spread his hands on the table. "What must I do to convince you? What will it take to earn your trust?"

"You can start by telling the truth," Yokum said flatly. "What do you hope to gain? As if I can't guess."

Fargo was watching Silvermane and Darnell. They were more likely to spot him than their bosses. Especially the hawk-eyed gunfighter. He was so intent on them, he failed to notice other men moving toward him until a walking lump of gristle pierced the din with a cry of warning.

"Look out, Mr. Yokum! It's the jasper you're after!"

Hell erupted. Fargo ducked down as guns crashed and holes mushroomed in the wall. He responded with a quick shot and the lump of gristle folded. But plenty of others were there to take his place. Screams, curses, and roars of outrage mixed in a cacophony of sound as panicked patrons ran in all directions. Quinby ducked under the table. Silvermane moved to shield Yokum with his own body.

Fargo should have known one or the other would have extra gunmen posted. Pinned against the wall as he was, he wouldn't last long. Suddenly a section to his right folded in on itself. Only it wasn't the wall, it was a door he hadn't realized was there.

A burly man armed with a shotgun stepped out. "What the hell is all the commotion about?"

Slipping behind him, Fargo sprinted down a narrow hall. He heard the man grunt at the impact of multiple bullets, heard the shotgun go off. The hall ended in a large storage room. Bottles lined shelves from floor to ceiling. Barrels were stacked in long rows.

"He went down here!"

Several gunmen had given chase. Fargo discouraged them with a slug that caught one in the knee and dropped him in his tracks. The sight of a back door spurred him into racing the length of the room. As he wrenched it open a bullet took a chip out of it.

Old crates, empty containers and bottles littered the alley. Fargo turned to the right, anxious to cover the three blocks to the hitch rail where the Ovaro was tied. Boots drummed in the room and he glanced back to see a head poke out. He fired again, buying himself enough time to reach the street.

His game of cat and mouse had gone awry. He was the hunted now instead of the hunter, and he was outnumbered twenty to one.

147

Curious pedestrians had stopped to stare toward the saloon. The gunfight had driven those inside into the street and general confusion reigned. Fargo wove in among them, slowing so as not to draw attention. He gained the opposite boardwalk and headed east.

Silvermane came out of the Havlock. "Spread out, boys! That yellow sidewinder can't have gotten far!"

Fargo halted. He was only two blocks from the Ovaro but he turned, replaced the empty cartridges, and strode toward the rectangle of light fronting the saloon. He wasn't more than twenty feet out when a gunman sparked to life.

"It's him! He's come back!"

A revolver glinted. Fargo already had the Colt cocked, and squeezed the trigger. A second gunman rushed out of the onlookers, headlong into a slug to the forehead. Fargo stepped over the body, bent to pick up the man's pistol, and advanced with a six-gun in each hand.

Two figures materialized out of the shadows. Fargo couldn't tell if they were more gunmen, or a couple of harmless townsmen or miners foolishly rushing up to see what all the shooting was about. So he didn't fire. His hesitation almost cost his life. The street rocked to gunfire, but in their reckless haste they rushed their shots. He didn't.

Silvermane waited on the boardwalk, his hands poised above his Smith and Wessons. It was a challenge. He was daring Fargo to confront him on equal terms, and Fargo accepted by striding purposefully toward him.

Then two things happened simultaneously: Spike Yokum appeared in the doorway behind Silvermane, and several gunmen rushed out of the alley, spied Fargo, and commenced spraying lead.

Dealing with the immediate threat took priority. Fargo shifted side on to make it harder for them to hit him and felt a slight tug at the fringe on his sleeve.

He fired both pistols. Two of the gunmen dropped. The third demonstrated why hired killers were notoriously unreliable: he wheeled and fled.

Fargo turned back toward the Havlock Saloon to find Silvermane gone. He took a step.

Marshal Darnell barreled into the night. His revolver was in his holster. Resting his hands on his hips, he surveyed the crowd, focusing on Fargo. "That will be quite enough! You are under arrest. Drop your guns and submit peacefully."

"Like hell."

Darnell had faith in the power of his badge. "We have laws in this town, mister, and you've broken a dozen or more. Don't make it difficult on yourself by bucking me. The good people of Nugget won't stand for having their duly appointed law officer assaulted."

Murmuring broke out, but Fargo stifled it by declaring, "What would the good people of Nugget say if they knew their marshal was in the mayor's hip pocket? What would they do if they learned their marshal tried to murder me today? That he has no scruples about breaking the law himself?"

Darnell's smug expression faded. "You don't have proof of any of that."

"All it takes is one look at you and they'll have all the proof they need," Fargo replied loudly enough so everyone within earshot heard.

The bluff had an effect. Some people were as transparent as glass, and Darnell was one of them. Backing up, he nervously licked his lips. "It would take more than that to convince a judge and jury."

"Why are you shying away?" Fargo demanded. "Conscience getting the better of you?" To those who were watching, he shouted, "Look at him! He's guilty as sin and it shows! Is this the kind of lawman you want?"

Again murmuring rippled like waves breaking on a shore. Marshal Darnell retreated to the door and was tensed like a blacktail buck about to bolt. "Now just hold on! All of you! You can't take this man's wild allegations seriously. I'm entitled to the benefit of the doubt like everyone else."

Fargo slowly advanced. "The law applies to you the same as the rest of us. I'll turn over my guns to these people if you'll do the same."

Darnell had the aspect of a cornered rat. He glanced right, then left, and when a couple of citizens moved forward, what little courage he possessed abandoned him. "Keep back! All of you! I'm the law here! You'll do as I say!"

"Unbuckle your gun belt," Fargo pressed him.

"You want my gun? Here it is!" Darnell's draw was clumsy and slow but that made him no less dangerous. His shot went high, and the next moment he was in the saloon.

Careful not to show himself, Fargo moved to a window. The saloon seemed empty but there hadn't been enough time for the lawman to reach the door on the far side. Stepping close to the bat-wings, he called out, "Give yourself up while you still can, Darnell. I don't want to kill you if I can help it." That was more for the crowd's benefit. He had no reservations about doing whatever it took. Lawmen gone bad weren't really lawmen at all. They were outlaws with badges.

"Don't come in! I'm warning you!"

The shout came from somewhere to his right. Crouching, Fargo crashed inside and went left. A shot cracked and a chair teetered. Reaching a table, Fargo flipped it over. Cards and chips went flying. Another bullet slammed into it as he flattened and crawled.

"Damn you!" Darnell raged. "Damn you to hell! We should have taken care of you the day you showed up."

As best Fargo could tell, the lawman was amid a cluster of tables along the east wall. He gained the bar and slowly rose to his hands and knees behind it.

"Cat got your tongue?" Darnell hollered. "The others lit out but not me. I'm not afraid of you! It'll be a clear-cut case of self-defense."

Setting the extra revolver on the floor, Fargo removed his hat and placed it on a shelf. He wrapped his fingers around an empty glass, then rose high enough to risk a quick glance. From this new angle he could see Darnell, crouched low.

"Show yourself!" The lawman was staring toward the overturned table. "Or are you yellow like Silvermane said?"

Fargo threw the glass toward the front of the saloon. At the *crash*, Darnell pivoted, desperately seeking a target. Fargo aimed at his gun hand, and fired.

Tom Darnell screeched like a knifed alley cat. Leaping to his feet, he clamped his right hand to his shirt. The hand was spouting blood like a geyser. Agony washing over him, he hissed through clenched teeth, "You shot me! You honest-to-God shot me! A duly appointed officer of the law!"

Replacing his hat, Fargo came out from behind the bar. He gripped the tin star. "Worms with badges don't deserve to wear them." Ripping it off, he tossed it across the room.

"I'll see you hang for this, you hear me?" Forgetting himself, Darnell lunged.

Fargo swatted him as he would a bug, then laced his fingers in the blood-soaked shirt. "You're still breathing only because I need to know where Quinby and Yokum went."

Darnell was one of those who never learned, a ten-year old in a grown man's body. "I'd like to see you make me!"

"Suit yourself." Seizing the wounded hand, Fargo squeezed.

A piercing shriek resulted. Darnell doubled over, blubbering and whining. "Stop! Stop! The mayor ordered me to arrest you, then ducked out the back! He didn't say where he was going!" Tears filled his eyes. "As for Yokum, all I know is that Silvermane wanted to stay and finish it but Yokum wouldn't let him. He mentioned something about catching a fish with the right bait, and they left."

What did that mean? Fargo wondered. Were they going after Marta again?

"What now?" Darnell mewed. "Are you fixing to finish what you've started?"

Fargo's contempt was boundless. "I won't waste the lead. Make yourself scarce. Light a shuck anywhere you want. Because if you're still in town this time tomorrow, they'll be planting you on boot hill."

"You're letting me live?" Relief lifted Darnell's spirits. "After I played you for a dunce and tried to kill you?"

"Don't remind me." Fargo spun the weasel around and planted his right boot at the appropriate spot. Darnell stumbled half the distance to the doors and smashed against a table. "If they ever have a sale on brains, buy some."

"Thank you, thank you, thank you!" Groveling like a whipped cur, Darnell dashed out.

Fargo reloaded again. The crowd outside had doubled in size with more arriving every minute as word spread. To avoid having a hundred and one questions thrown at him, he went out the back and down the alley. Few noticed him make a beeline for the Ovaro. Once he forked leather, he brought the stallion to a gallop. The Tumbleweed Hotel was his destination but he had gone only four blocks when he glanced to his left and saw a garish sign announcing the Motherlode, the saloon that belonged to Spike Yokum.

On an impulse Fargo reined toward it, and slowed. The street was filled with celebrants. Shucking the Henry, he laid it across the pommel. Movement on a rooftop registered and he reined up. A hat appeared, then the head of the man wearing it, and finally the rifle he was holding. Which he pressed to his shoulder to aim.

To the west the blazing sun was on its downward arc. It painted the horizon in bright hues of red and orange. It also silhouetted the bushwhacker. Fargo centered the Henry and went for a heart shot. He had to hike the barrel a hair, but compensating for elevation was second nature to someone who had spent much of his adult life roaming mountain ranges from Canada to Mexico. The blast pealed like thunder.

Almost instantly another rifleman reared up on a rooftop on the right. A bullet smacked the dirt near the Ovaro's front legs.

Fargo worked the Henry's lever and fired. He had hoped to avoid a raging gun battle in the streets. There were too many bystanders. Yokum, though, had no such compunctions.

The revelers were fleeing. Some of the women and children were screaming, but for the most part their flight was as orderly as could be expected. Many sought sanctuary in adjacent buildings.

Swinging to the ground, Fargo ran to a water trough and dropped to his knees behind it.

Mayor Jonathan Quinby appeared in the doorway of Yokum's saloon. He had his arms over his head and was gnawing on his lower lip as if he were starved and it was the only food available. His bowler was missing, his suit rumpled, his shirt partway out. Someone had roughed him up, by the look of things. "Don't shoot!" he bawled. "I'm unarmed!"

Shadows flitted across the saloon windows. Suddenly a pane was shattered by a rifle butt.

"Fargo? Can you hear me out there?" Wisely, Spike Yokum didn't show himself. "I'm willing to talk if you're willing to listen."

"The time for talk is past."

"How would you like to ride out of town with twenty thousand dollars in your pocket? All you have to do is agree to go our separate ways with no more gunplay. I never wanted it to come to this. You're the one who started killing my men without cause."

Fargo shook his head in disgust. When it came to lying, Yokum and Quinby were peas in the same pod. "I'd say kidnaping Marta Endelstrom and planning to use her to kill me was cause enough."

"Who told you that? Was it her? Didn't it ever occur to you that she was wrapping you around her finger for her own benefit? She's not exactly a saint, you know. She's hoping you'll fill me with lead so she can get her hands on my money."

The idea was preposterous. Fargo knew it, and Yokum knew it, too. In which case Yokum had to be up to something. Stalling, perhaps. Fargo scanned the rooftops but saw no one.

"How about if I send the mayor out to discuss it?" Yokum proposed. "He's unarmed, so don't go shooting him. All you have to do is listen."

Quinby stepped into the street, his arms still up, his face a mask of pure and total fear. He was so scared, he wobbled as he walked, as if his legs no longer functioned. They moved stiffly, like twin rake handles, first one, then the other, his shoes practically dragging in the dirt. He began whimpering and stopped gnawing on his lower lip long enough to say, "Please don't kill me! I don't want to die."

Fargo knew Yokum was up to something but for the life of him he couldn't figure out what. Sending the mayor out was pointless. There was nothing to discuss. It had to be more stalling on Yokum's part. To what end? What did Yokum hope to accomplish?

"I don't want to do this," Quinby sobbed. "They're making me." He gave a start and jerked forward.

Almost as if he had been pushed. Fargo stared at the gap between the mayor's chubby legs. The next time one moved, there was a hint, the barest suggestion, of a patch of black attached to it. Of a shadow where there shouldn't be a shadow. Of a second leg moving at the same time as Quinby's leg. Someone was behind him, goading him on. Someone smaller than Quinby, someone dressed in black. That was when Fargo realized the mayor's abject fright wasn't directed at him, but at the man using him as a shield.

Fargo let them come a little closer, then commented, "And you had the gall to call *me* yellow, Silvermane? You're the one hiding behind that worthless gob of spit."

The mayor halted. Or, rather, was jerked to a halt.

"I told Yokum this wouldn't work," Silvermane declared.

A revolver cracked. Fargo dropped below the trough but the shot wasn't intended for him. When he rose up again, Mayor Jonathan Quinby was swaying like a tree in a gale, his eyes rolling into their sockets, a fair chunk of his head gone.

Silvermane had stepped into the open, his Smith and Wessons in his hands. He twirled them into their studded holsters, then slapped Quinby on the back. The mayor thudded to earth. "This wasn't my brainstorm, I'll have you know. I'd rather finish this man to man. Just the two of us. As it was always meant to be."

Fargo slowly stood, his hands at his sides. "The problem with being a puppet is that someone else is always pulling your strings."

Silvermane shrugged. "It pays well, and that's all I'm interested in." He flexed his fingers a few times. "Let's get this over with. Yokum promised me a five thousand dollar bonus for dropping you."

"It will take a bigger man than you."

For a span of ten heartbeats Silvermane was rigid with resentment. Then he grinned, and his hands flew.

So did Fargo's. They cleared leather at the same

split second but his Colt roared a fraction sooner. His side seared with pain and he cocked the Colt to fire again but it wasn't necessary.

The eyes of the man in black had gone blank. Gore oozed from a pink hole between them. His legs convulsed, and he fell across the mayor.

Fargo glanced down at his shirt. He had been creased, nothing more. Leaden bees reminded him it wasn't over yet, and he looked up to discover Spike Yokum and three gunmen charging from the saloon. Spinning, Fargo dived. He wrapped his fingers around the Henry, heaved up and worked the lever as rapidly as he could, seven, eight, nine shots in all. When he stopped, four more bodies were waiting for the undertaker.

Suddenly Fargo heard the rush of footsteps behind him. Another gunman, he thought, and rotated.

Marta threw herself at him and clung fast, her breath warm on his neck. "I was too worried to stay put! I had to come find you." She gazed at the string of dead. "Are we safe at last?"

"One of us is." Grinning, Fargo lifted her into his arms and carried her to the Ovaro. "Climb on. We're going to the hotel."

"Mercy me!" Marta's smile was ripe with promise. "Just what do you have in mind?"

LOOKING FORWARD!
The following is the opening
section from the next novel in the exciting
Trailsman series from Signet:

THE TRAILSMAN #262

BADLAND BLOODBATH

The Badlands, 1861—
Where the Iron Horse carries many to a new life—
and some to a hard death.

A hen pheasant abruptly whirred up from a rocky gorge well below Skye Fargo's position. He aimed his slitted gaze in that direction, mindful that he was conveniently skylined for any shooters hidden below.

"Spot any trouble, Mr. Fargo?" called out Owen Maitland from behind.

Maitland, a surveyor hired by the Northwestern Short Line Railroad, stood stooped over behind his Gunter's chain, sighting track bed for a new spur between Laramie and the nearby settlement of Bear Creek.

"No Sioux or Cheyennes close by," Fargo replied,

still studying the gorge below as he reined in beside a clear, sand-bottom creek. He threw off and then dropped the bridle so his Ovaro could drink. "But I spotted a she-grizz with cubs foraging not far from here. Keep your eyes peeled."

"I ain't scairt of no grizz," boasted Danny Ford, the green but likable kid who had been hired to hold the sticks for Maitland. "Mr. Fargo's got him a Henry rifle."

"You'd need a buffalo gun to drop a grizzly. Besides, I don't shoot anything or anybody if I can avoid it, Danny," Fargo replied absently. He was still watching that gorge below them while he stripped off his saddle and spread the sweat-soaked saddle blanket out to dry in the hot sun.

He was a tall, rangy, muscle-corded man with lake-blue eyes in a bearded and weather-tanned face. Several strings in the fringes of his buckskins were black with old blood. His eyes shifted to read the horizon, searching for dust puffs or reflections, looking for motion, not shapes. Then his attention returned to the gorge, which he hadn't searched since early morning.

Maybe that was a mistake. . . .

Fargo definitely did not welcome the gut hunch he was feeling right now. He could find signs where most men saw only bare hardpan. Once, in a howling sandstorm, he had even tracked an unshod Comanche pony across New Mexico's blistering Staked Plain, a baked alkali hell drier than a year-old cow chip.

But the man some called the Trailsman had also learned to heed this "goose tickle" he felt now—a cold prickling on the back of his neck which only came just before all hell broke loose.

"Brother!" exclaimed Maitland, pausing to swipe at his sweaty brow with a handkerchief. "What I'd give right now to be drowning in an ocean of lemonade. That sun is hot as a branding iron."

Fargo, too, had been feeling the hot weight of the sun for several hours now. It was hard to believe there had been a thin powdering of frost on the grass when he rolled out of his blanket at dawn. Spring was a highly notional season in the Wyoming Territory.

He glimpsed a yellow coyote slinking off through the gorge below, not far from where the hen had flown up. Fargo relaxed a little, though he resolved to scout out that gorge again when the Ovaro had drunk and rested a little.

Fargo had been in the saddle since sunup, and his thighs and tailbone were sore. But even worse than the tiresome patrolling through rough terrain was his irritation with himself for accepting railroad money. He had been forced to find paying work for awhile—hell, he didn't have two nickels to rub together. He could hunt for his meals and sleep under the stars, but no amount of good trailcraft could provide ammunition, coffee or a glass of beer. Only cold, hard cash.

But by now he knew the sickening pattern. Guns had gone from flintlock to cap and ball to the self-contained cartridge, and through most of that change the West had remained the same. However, the shining times were over.

Soon enough Maitland would be followed by track bed levelers, the pounding of spike mauls. First would come the early boomers, profiting quick and moving on. Then would come the cities with their foolish laws and rules so that a city dweller could never be truly free. "Cussed syphillization" as the old mountain men used to call it when a pristine wilderness began to settle up. The railroad plutocrats, the land-grabbers and strip miners had already washed in on a flood of eastern and foreign capital, a flood that was drowning out the strong-heart songs of the fur traders and Plains warriors.

Maitland had stopped work to build himself a smoke. He watched the Trailsman with friendly curiosity. The surveyor was a small, thin, middle-aged man wearing a boiled shirt, his sturdy canvas trousers tucked into calfskin boots. He had removed his high, glazed paper collar hours ago.

"Mr. Fargo," he remarked, "you do an excellent job of protecting me and Danny. But if you'll pardon my saying so, I get the distinct impression you'd rather be someplace else."

"This is fine country, and you and Danny are pleasant company," Fargo assured him honestly.

Fargo's pinto stallion lifted its nose from the creek, snorted, then stared toward the gorge below, sensitive nostrils quivering as they caught a scent.

Could be that coyote, Fargo told himself. But he felt the goose tickle again, like lice crawling against his scalp. He slipped the bridle back on, but the tired Ovaro resisted the bit.

"All right, old campaigner, a few more minutes," Fargo surrendered, grateful for the rest himself.

Maitland finished rolling his smoke, then expertly quirled the ends. He turned away from the wind to light it.

"If you can put up with this nursing job," he told Fargo, "the Santa Fe and Topeka Railroad is sending me down into the ass end of west Texas next. You're welcome to come along."

Fargo squatted on his heels and idly picked his teeth with a weed, his profile half in shadow under the slanted brim of his hat. Just west of this mostly flat tableland, the Laramie Mountains rose in ascending folds, the highest peaks still wearing ermine capes of snow. Due north, past the railroad tracks below and the rocky gorge beyond, the slopes were golden yellow with arrowroot blossoms. Here and there he spotted bright red splashes of the plant called Indian paintbrush.

Beautiful country, all right. But he glanced toward the east, where the short-grass prairie rolled on to the horizon, prime graze land. A stock tank was visible perhaps two miles distant. He had ridden past it earlier and seen a few mottled longhorns drinking— including some of the first seed bulls driven onto northern ranges from the cattle-rich *brasada* country of Texas.

Progress, some called it. Whatever its name, it dogged him like an afternoon shadow, always there when he glanced over his shoulder.

"Thanks for the offer," he finally replied. "But as soon as I'm not so light in the pockets, I'll be drifting on."

Maitland shrugged. "No harm in asking. I s'pose some fellows are just one-man outfits. Anyhow, won't be too long now and my rheumatism will have me all seized up in the hinges. Then I can retire to the liar's bench and brag how I tamed the West."

Danny had overheard them and now came running over. He was tall and gangly, with a wild shock of red hair, a snaggly-toothed grin and pants gone through at the knees.

"Can I go to Texas with you, Mr. Maitland?" he demanded in a welter of excitement. "I ain't got no ma or pa, so it's nobody's say-so if I go."

Fargo grinned at the kid. Danny spent most of his time in Bear Creek, mucking out stables and catching rats. Holding sticks for the railroad surveyor was the high point of his young life.

"What about Mr. Hupenbecker at the livery?" Maitland asked. "I thought he's your boss?"

"Aww, that's cowplop," Danny insisted. "Lookit Mr. Fargo, nobody tells him where he can work, do they?"

"Let it alone, Danny," Fargo advised the kid. "It's no big adventure to find yourself with the sun going low and no supper."

Or to constantly have gun sights notched on you, Fargo thought, deciding it was high time to scout out that gorge again.

This time his faithful Ovaro took the bit easily. Fargo was shaking burrs out of the saddle blanket when a steam whistle suddenly shrilled in the distance. The lonesome sound trailed off into silence except for the faint, rhythmic chuffing of the approaching locomotive, still out of sight from their position.

"The two-twenty from Cheyenne," Maitland announced.

"That's the orphan train!" Danny exclaimed. "And that pretty newspaper lady is with 'em!"

Even Fargo, who hadn't read a newspaper in weeks, knew about the much-ballyhooed orphan train from back east. Damnedest thing he'd ever heard of. Evidently, Manhattan had become overrun with street urchins, and the publicity-hungry politician "Boss" Tweed had come up with a novel solution: Load the orphans aboard trains and send them out west, where settlers could look them over and pick the ones they wanted to come live with them. Fargo figured some of those unfortunate waifs would end up ill-used, turned into work horses. But others would find loving families. Almost anything was better than being abandoned to the mean city streets back east.

"What pretty lady might that be?" Fargo inquired as he centered his saddle.

"Gal named Kristen McKenna," Maitland replied. "Writes for the *New York Herald,* and I hear she's pretty as four aces. She's riding along to do stories on each kid that's picked by a family."

"Never heard of her," Fargo said, cinching his latigos.

Maitland's tone turned sly and teasing. "Then it sounds like she's about the *only* female that's escaped your notice. I heard about that little set-to last Saturday night at Lilly Ketchum's sporting house in Laramie. How many of Sheriff Bolton's tinhorn deputies did you toss through the windows?"

Fargo feigned pure innocence. "All I remember rightly was all these starmen who kept running into my fists. Just clumsy, I expect."

"You'd best watch that bunch," Maitland suggested tactfully. "They're a secret ring, you ask me. A bunch of back-scratching cousins. Bolton's one of those bribes or bullets sheriffs and he's related to most of his deputies *and* the judge. Those boys run Bear Creek like private property and tend to put the noose before the gavel. And it 'pears to me there's more and more rough fellows in this area eager to pin the no-good sign on you, Mr. Fargo. Especially the ones whose wives and sweethearts have heard of you."

Fargo stepped into a stirrup and pushed up and over. He tugged rein and wheeled right, heading down the face of the hill.

"Wives and sweethearts are safe with me," he called back over his shoulder. "Why toss your loop over branded stock when there's plenty of free-range mavericks?"

"You're telling me Lilly's sparkling doxies are *free*?"

"Damn, I wasn't s'posed to tell you paying men," Fargo shouted, and he heard Maitland laughing behind him.

Again the steam whistle shrilled, much closer now.

Excerpt from *BADLAND BLOODBATH*

The 2:20 from Laramie suddenly hove into view around the shoulder of Flint-Covered Mountain, the locomotive's diamond stack emitting huge, dark clouds of coal smoke. It was dramatically black against a vast, cloudless sky the pure blue of a gas flame.

The engine pulled a tender, four wooden coaches, and a caboose. Fargo glimpsed curious, pale young faces peering out of the windows. He booted the Ovaro up from a walk to a trot, figuring he could easily cross the tracks before the train reached him.

Less than a heartbeat later, things started happening ten ways a second.

With a huge, cracking boom, a section of track a hundred yards in front of the Trailsman suddenly exploded, ripped apart, and flew into the air. Fargo and his mount were showered in a descending cloud of dirt, rocks, and splintered ties.

The orphan train, moving along at thirty miles per hour, was only a few hundred yards from the blast area. The engineer could only throttle back, for the brakes were controlled by men stationed atop the passenger cars. Fargo, still wiping dirt from his eyes, watched the brakemen leap to their brake wheels and desperately start turning them.

Shots erupted from the rocky gorge north of the tracks. Fargo watched one of the brakemen, blood pluming from a chest hit, tumble dead to the ground beside the tracks. Another brakeman whipped a dragoon pistol out from under his duster and returned fire. He was hit a second later, dropping between two coaches. Fargo winced at the man's short, horrific scream before the train wheels crushed him.

When Fargo spotted masked men boiling out from the gorge, he whipped his Henry out of its saddle scabbard and levered a round into the chamber, throwing the weapon into his shoulder socket. Before he could even get a bead on one of them, however, withering gunfire erupted in his direction.

Like a sledgehammer blow, a round thwacked into his heavy leather gunbelt. Although the bullet failed to completely penetrate the thick leather, a white-hot pain grated in his left hip. Only his strong leg muscles kept him from being wiped out of the saddle.

Rounds filled the air around him, some passing so close they sounded like angry hornets. Fargo could see at least five men, all armed with rifles, and he knew they'd shoot him and the Ovaro to mattress stuffings if he foolishly kept charging across the open ground.

He rolled out of the saddle, tugging the reins as he fell to wheel the pinto around.

"Hee *yah!*" he shouted, slapping its glossy rump to send the well trained Ovaro back over the hill.

Fargo made himself so flat he felt like he was making love to the ground. A glance over his shoulder revealed Maitland and Danny, frozen with shock.

"Don't stand there with your thumbs up your sitters!" he shouted at them. "That's lead they're tossing at us! Cover down!"

He had no time to see if they followed his order, for just then the train hit the expanse of blown track. It had slowed considerably, but not enough to keep from jackknifing before it crashed at the bottom of the embankment, every car derailed except the caboose.

Two of the men in the gorge kept Fargo pinned while the rest went to work quickly and efficiently. At gunpoint they herded the dazed and shaken passengers, mostly kids, toward two buckboards waiting at the mouth of the gorge. When Fargo started to draw a bead, one of the men below picked up a little girl

165

in a calico frock and gray sunbonnet. He held his gun to her head, and a furious Fargo got the message. Feeling helpless and enraged, he lowered his Henry.

But the dry-gulchers didn't take just kids. Fargo watched one of them briefly struggling with a wheat blond beauty wearing a velvet-trimmed traveling suit. Even from his present position Fargo saw she had cheeks like fall apples and a bodice ready to rip from the strain of her full breasts.

Her lacquered straw hat, with its gay blue ribbon and bright ostrich feather, went sailing off into the wind when her captor suddenly slugged her, knocking her out. Anger and frustration simmering within, Fargo could only helplessly watch as the woman was tossed into one of the buckboards among crying and terrified children. He wasn't about to raise his rifle and get one of those kids killed.

The buckboards disappeared into the gorge. Fargo rolled to one side and shoved down his buckskin trousers to glance at his wound. No blood, just one hell of a bruise already coloring up. He pushed to his feet, whistling for the Ovaro.

Danny was the first to speak, his jaw falling open in pure astonishment. "Jiminy! Didja *see* that? Cripes, who was them men?"

"A litter of prairie rats, that's who," Fargo replied, catching hold of the Ovaro's bridle and stepping into leather. The stallion had whiffed blood from below and pranced nervously.

Maitland, pale as chalk, found his voice. "You going after them, Mr. Fargo?"

He shook his head. "Not now, or they'll be tossing dead kids off those buckboards. There's no other reason to grab those kids than a fat ransom from the railroad. It won't matter if their trail goes cold, a blind hog could track them. Right now there's dead and wounded below to tend to. C'mon.''

But Maitland and Danny were still shocked and just stood there, staring in disbelief at the mangled train and dead bodies.

"Nerve up, you two!" he shouted in a tone they couldn't ignore. "This ain't some dog and pony show, there's folks down there who need help.''

Both men leaped into action as Fargo raced downhill toward the disaster scene. He paused only once, to lean down and pluck the woman's beribboned hat out of the grass.

It still bore a pleasant aroma of honeysuckle shampoo. He tucked it into one of his saddle panniers and promised himself he'd be returning it to that ample-bosomed beauty real soon.